Sandy Times

By Giselle Lumas

SANDY TIMES
By Giselle Lumas

Original Copyright ©1994 Giselle Lumas
Revision Copyright ©2011 Giselle Lumas

Giselle Lumas

Email the author at GiselleLumas@gmail.com
Visit www.gisellelumas.com and www.gigilumas.com

More books by Giselle Lumas

Adult Romance:
Tug of Love
Melody's Blues
Truth or Dare: A Love Story
A Holiday Bet
Alida's Way
Captain of My Heart
The Captain's Son
The Captain's Love
Before the Christmas Wedding

Young Adult Fiction:
Journal of a Cymbal Player: Freshman Year

Science Fiction/Fantasy:
Malique's Quest
The World Through a Shaded Eye: Lani's Mission

Cozy Mysteries:
Spilling the Jellybeans (Beach City Cozy Mysteries: Patsy- Book One)
Santa's Helper Bytes the Dust (Beach City Cozy Mysteries: Patsy- Book Two)
Nailed It! (Beach City Cozy Mysteries: Patsy- Book Three)
Food Fight! (Beach City Cozy Mysteries: Patsy- Book Four)
A Nutty Holiday Drama (Beach City Cozy Mysteries: Patsy- Book Five)

Children's Book:
THE SUPERHERO WHO SAVED CHRISTMAS (Co-author Tyler Lumas)

Collection of Romantic Short Stories:

Love Stories Short and Sweet: Some with a Little Tart

Poetry:
Poetic Thoughts
When Peddles Fall (More Poetic Thoughts)

Coming soon…

Romance:
Jazz's Time

Cozy Mystery:
Beach City Cozy Mystery: Patsy- Book Six

Dedication

To my sister: Patrice Long
For always being there even when she was miles away!

To my brother: Brien Gauthier
For always cheering me on!

Roving in a path
others advised me to take
Don't want to disappoint
struggle and desire to achieve and please
There is a gash in my heart
a void in my soul
Wish I could see
which way I should go
Things aren't so black and white
It's grainy and beige

These are sandy times.

CHAPTER ONE: "Should I introduce myself?"

I was watering the front lawn. Actually, I was just standing with the hose in my hand and letting the water go wherever it wanted to go. I wasn't paying any attention. If I had been, I would have noticed that my black canvas shoes were constantly being rained on. My attention was focused on my neighbors across the street. They were new here. In fact, they were still in the process of moving in. A U-Haul truck just pulled up in their driveway. They must have a lot of furniture because that was the third time I had seen the truck.

I didn't make it a habit of spying on people. I didn't! It's just that I really and truly didn't like the people moving in across the street. How could I not like people I hadn't even met? Easy. They were moving in on my turf. Or what had once been my turf. Okay, it had never really been my turf. It was just that someone who meant so much to me used to live there. In a way, you could almost say that I lived there with him since I was there almost every single day. Now he lived on the other side of the country.

He was in Atlanta, Georgia to be precise. He was probably freezing. I was in sunny Southern California, wearing cutoffs and a magenta t-shirt with my curly out of control hair pulled back into a messy ponytail. You would never guess it was the middle of November.

I felt that if the new neighbors hadn't been so eager to buy Jerry's house he would still be here.

I watched a ten-year-old boy with red hair and skinny legs attempt to carry a box bigger than him. Some blond headed guy stopped him. I noticed that the woman, I assumed the wife, was pregnant I also noticed that she was moving her mouth. I strained my ears so I could hear what she was saying.

"That box goes in the living room. And Jake, remember to bend your knees when picking up the boxes. We don't need to make another trip to the chiropractor?" She seemed like a nag. She was wearing a blue denim jumpsuit with a white T-shirt and white tennis shoes. Her brunette hair was cut short. I guessed you could say boyish short.

My attention went back to what they were saying, "? but Dad, I wanted that room! How come Jamie always gets her way? She's not even here?" He seemed like a brat. They won't catch me babysitting him anytime soon. The three of them disappeared into the house. I heard the door slam shut.

They hadn't even noticed me standing there. They didn't say hello or introduce themselves. Hmmm… Was I supposed to do that? Hmmm? maybe tomorrow.

Suddenly I became aware that my socks were soaking wet. Half of the lawn was dry while the other half had a nice big muddy puddle. Oops.

Just then I heard the front door behind me open. Uh oh. My stomach began to get upset. It was my sister. My heart raced into overdrive when I heard her deep raspy voice ask me in her typical accusatory tone, "Sandy, what are you doing?"

Even though I knew she was there, I still jumped from the sound of her voice. My eyes were glossed over and looked guilty even though I didn't do anything wrong. Ever since we were little, my sister had a way of making me feel like I did something wrong even when I didn't. Yes, I overwatered the lawn but that was it. "What does it look like I am doing?" I asked defensively.

"Killin' my lawn," Gina walked to the faucet and turned it off. "You know good and well that we have sprinklers. Now tell me the truth." She had her hands on her hips and appeared to be ready for combat.

I dropped the hose and made a dash for the house. I knew what she wanted from me, but I wasn't going to give it to her. She wanted me to cry on her shoulder, but I refused to. As I ran, little bubbles formed from my shoes. When I finally made it inside, I slipped on the ceramic tile and landed on my behind. I winced from the blow to my ego and my throbbing bottom. I sat there for a moment. I figured since I was down, I might as well remove my shoes and peel off my socks. Yuck. My feet were slimy and wrinkly. I wiggled my toes. I admired my French pedicure momentarily. I painted them myself earlier in the day and had even pasted little sticky flowers I had bought from Target a few days before.

My sister was right behind me. She didn't see me fall. Good. "You know, it's okay to cry, Sandy?

"I already have," finally admitting to her as I stood up. I left the shoes and socks by the door per my brother-in-law's previous anal instructions so as not to track a bunch of dirt on his newly ceramic tiled floor. "I'll have the rent money in two days," I said, hoping to change the subject. My sister wasn't only my sister, but she was also my landlord. I paid her rent for the use of one bedroom, one-third of the kitchen, use of bathroom and the laundry room. I also paid her an extra fifty dollars a month so she wouldn't tell me what to do.

"Don't try to change the subject. I know you are still hurting. I know how much you loved him. It was wrong of him to just up and leave like that. He didn't give you much notice and?"

"Gina," I interrupted her, "If you don't mind, I would like to forget about Mr. Jerry Jones! So, like I said, I will have the money in two days." We were still standing near the front door.

"You'd better, or you'll find yourself on the next bus back to Mom's," she said with a smile. I swore that was her favorite threat. She loved having a hold on me! "But I'm not finished talking about Jerry." The constant lingering bitterness rose inside of me. Yes, I was grateful for her to allow me to stay with her. I was extremely grateful but at the same time I was angry for not having any other real choice.

I turned away from her and started walking toward the kitchen. "You go on ahead and talk about him without me. I am going to the kitchen?" I didn't wait for her answer. I was already in the kitchen. Of course, as always, Gina was right behind me. "You need to let it out, girl. You're going to get sick. The way you just hold things in?" I attempted to shoo her away like a fly. The more I tried to shoo her the closer she came to me.

"I told you I already did the crying thing," I declared, not looking at her. I opened the refrigerator and bent down to get the container of fruit salad. I deliberately bent further than necessary so that the only image Gina could see was my butt. I was hoping she'd get the message when I swayed my hips side to side to give my butt a wiggle and jiggle effect.

Well, she noticed my butt alright. She viewed it as a target for her right foot. She kicked me and my head slammed into the milk. I heard her laughing. In between giggles, she managed to sputter; "Now you need to do the talking thing."

I didn't know how it happened. Maybe it was the humiliation of Gina pressing her foot against my butt. When I stood up, I found tears rushing down my cheeks, and I started wailing like a three-year-old.

Gina's laughter subsided. She turned me around so that I faced her and gave me a big hug. I needed it. I didn't know what was happening to me. I couldn't stop crying. Gina finally let me go. She led me to the table and handed me a pile of napkins.

I blew my nose. It was an ugly sight to see. "Are... are? y? you? you? satis... s? fied?" Sniff. Sniff.

14

"I'll be more satisfied if I could get Derrick on the next flight to Atlanta. He could kick Jerry on the opposite side where I kicked you.

"Who kicked who" I heard Derrick ask. Derrick was Gina's husband. He wasn't supposed to be home right now. He was supposed to be working overtime at the hospital. Dang it, I didn't want anyone to see me have a nervous breakdown. Gina waved her hand, signaling him to go away. He went away mumbling some profanity and something about women. Gina ignored him. I blew my nose one more time. I knew my face was probably splotchy, and I could feel my lips swelling to enormous proportions. My eyes were probably red by now, and my eyelids were feeling puffy. I probably looked like a sick blowfish.

"Sandy, are you ready to talk about it? Are you prepared to tell me the whole story?" Gina asked gently as she rubbed my back.

My eyebrows nearly touched one another. "I can't."

"Yes, you can."

She was right. I could have easily told her why Jerry left so quickly. It was just so hard. Gina didn't know he was married. He had been married for the two years I was seeing him. I wasn't a home wrecker. He just failed to tell me that bit of information. He finally revealed it when I found a "For Sale" sign jabbed into his front lawn.

"Sandy talk to me."

My hands trembled as I wiped my eyes with another napkin and took a deep breath.

"There isn't much to tell, Gina. All I can say is that he went to Atlanta to be with his wife." It felt good to let it out.

"Wife!" Gina shouted as she jumped out of her seat. She began to pace the kitchen floor. "You've been screwing somebody's husband for the past two years! How could you do something like that?"

My ears started to ring. My own sister had already labeled me as a cheap tramp. She didn't think that maybe I didn't know he was married. "Gina, I didn't?"

She stopped pacing, looked at me and finally asked with concern in her eyes, "How long have you known he was married?" I could see that her brown eyes were filled with a glimmer of hope. She was hoping that her little sister wasn't a horny home wrecker.

I was tempted to tell her that I knew from the very beginning just to make her mad. But instead, I told her the truth. "Just before escrow closed," I managed to mumble and sniffed.

My sister's angry, disappointed expression transformed into the most sympathetic expression I had ever seen her wear. She collapsed into a chair and scooted it next to me. "Oh, Sandy? I'm sorry. I know you're hurting. I thought you two were going to be married. I know you thought the same. But he turns out to be married?" She stopped talking for a second as if she realized something for the first time. "I've never seen his wife. He never wore a wedding, band."

"His wife lives in Atlanta. Three years ago, he received a promotion out here. She wanted to stay in Georgia, but he wanted to leave. So, they separated." I bit the side of my lip. Talking about it helped. "So, for the past two years he'd go visit her whenever he had a vacation. Apparently on the last vacation they conceived a baby. So?"

Gina let out a gasp then said, "That's why when he came back last time, he was so cruel towards you, isn't it?"

I hadn't even thought of that. When he came back from Georgia after Easter, I had met him at the airport. I was smiling and full of anticipation with a small bouquet of flowers for him. I couldn't wait to see him as I waited in baggage claim. When he saw me, though, he frowned and asked, "What are you doing here? Did I tell you to pick me up?"

16

Derrick interrupted my thoughts. "It'll be alright, Sandy."

Both Gina and I looked up. "You were listening?" I asked.

"Yeah, I couldn't help it. I wanted to know why I was being kicked out of my kitchen." He patted me on the shoulder and said, "Don't worry. I know plenty of single guys who will treat you right. Whenever you want to meet one of them, just let me know. Okay?" He was no longer in his work clothes but now in his over worn dark blue denim shorts and white tank top.

"Yeah, Derrick." Gina's eyes brightened. "Hook her up baby."

"Jacob just might be good for Sandy."

"Jacob?" Gina asked with her mouth twisted to one side. "Who is Jacob? He'd better be somebody good."

"Hello," I said. "Excuse me. Sandy is still in the room." I was annoyed that the two of them were trying to run my love life. It was interesting to see how they could quickly jump from one man to another.

"I'm sorry," Gina said as she patted me on the back. She looked back at Derrick and asked, "Is he cute?" She seemed to have a glazed look in her eyes.

"Babe, I'm not setting you up with him. Remember, you're married? You married me." Derrick spun around as if he were modeling and then flexed his arms. He gave an exaggerated smile that flashed his famous dimples. Gina waved her hands at him as if to say he was dismissed. How Derrick had put up with her for seven years, I didn't know.

"Gina, I don't want to go out with any man for at least two years." I had decided when I woke up this morning that two years would give me the right amount of time to get over Jerry. I figured I would have graduated college by then or at least I hoped. I also thought I would be at least a year into my wonderful, mysterious career by then. Of

17

course, I still didn't know what my career would be but hopefully I would figure it out by then.

"Two years?" Gina repeated softly. I could tell Gina was only half listening to my statement. I knew it would take a moment longer for it to register completely. "TWO YEARS!" Now that was more like it.

"Sandy?" She shook her head, and as she did so, the braids in her hair knocked against her cheek. "I hate to tell you this, but? Jerry wasn't all that. He was fine and smart but?" She put her hands on top of mine. Her light brown eyes looked into my dark brown eyes, and she said sincerely, "the man stank."

I laughed. I couldn't help it. "He did not?" Why I defended him, I did not know.

We argued for a while on the body odor subject. Finally, it ended with Gina saying, "I'm going to send him a bar of soap for Christmas. What's his address?" Gina stood up and walked to one of the drawers in the kitchen. She opened the one that was on the telephone. She pulled out her black velvet clothed phone book and blue ink pen.

I recited his address. I couldn't believe I knew Jerry's new address by heart. He had given it to me in case I ever needed anything. Of course, he said he'd prefer it if I never used it. I felt angry with myself. Why should I feel so sad and lonely? Why should I be boohooing over a man who lied to me the whole time we were supposedly dating each other? I bared my soul to him and where did it leave me? Here I was twenty-three years old, still in college, sales clerk and mooching off my sister and brother-in-law. I hated it.

Derrick returned holding a sports magazine in his hand. "Sandy, you might want to change clothes and brush your hair. You might want to slick back all the hair sticking out of what you call a ponytail. Use some gel and a bristle brush. Oh, and while you are at it, put some makeup on and… and… please, brush your teeth, floss, and use some

18

mouthwash, use some of that whitening mouthwash, you know the one I'm talking about, right? Gina, you bought her some mouthwash the other day when we were at Target, right?"

I blinked my eyes, not believing what I was hearing. Not only did he tell me when to clean my room; when to do the dishes; when to pay rent; and who I should or shouldn't go out with, but now he was telling me how to look. I bit my lower lip hard. I was hoping it would prevent me from saying something I'd regret later.

Gina giggled as she watched me. "Girl, your face is turning colors. Let it out. Don't hold it in. Tell him off?" Gina encouraged me.

Instead, I took a deep breath and clenched my fist. Ever since the day I met Derrick he felt he had to play the big brother role. He loved it. I think he enjoyed seeing me upset. "Jacob will be here in about an hour."

"What?" Both Gina and I asked in unison.

My head was beginning to hurt. I started rubbing my temples with my index fingers. Didn't I pay them an extra fifty dollars a month so they wouldn't tell me what to do? What was going on? I wanted a refund, that was for sure.

I continued massaging my temples and closed my eyes. Why was my heart beating so fast? Why was I feeling a tiny bit glad that this Jacob guy was coming over? Shouldn't I be upset? I frowned although my insides were smiling.

"I talked to him a few weeks ago at work. We ended up talking about you, and I showed him a picture of you. He wanted to meet you then, but you were still dating Jerry." Derrick casually strolled over to the sink. He grabbed a glass from the beige drain board and filled it with cold water. He strolled over to the refrigerator and reached up to the cabinet just above the fridge. He grabbed the container of colon cleanse and placed it on the counter top. He measured two tablespoons of the non-flavored super fiber and dumped it into the glass. I could hear the clink, clink of the glass as he stirred the spoon around.

"While the two of you were talking, I called Jacob. He's coming over for dinner," Derrick said matter-of-factly. He gulped down the bowel moving liquid in just a few seconds time. I made a face as he put the glass down. It was his ritual. Come home, change into shorts and a tank top then immediately drink a glass of colon cleanser. I rubbed my belly as if I would be the one to feel the effects.

"Excuse me," Gina said, "I am not cooking for someone I haven't even met."

"Babe, trust me. I wouldn't want you to," Derrick said.

CHAPTER TWO: "I'm a natural kind of woman."

Gina forced me to stay in her bathroom while she attempted to do my hair. She had already straightened my usually frizzy out of control curly hair with her flat iron, but now she wanted to add a little curl. She grabbed the curling iron and spat on it to see if it was hot. I heard it fizz. "Did you have to do that?"

"What do you want me to do? Feel it with my hand?" The bathroom wasn't big enough for the two of us. "Why won't you get extensions anyway? It would be easier to take care of."

"Gina?"

Just then I heard the doorbell ring. I stared at Gina's reflection in the mirror. She was looking right back at me. "He's here," we both said in a panicked whisper.

I looked like crap. I was still wearing cut-off blue jeans and a rose colored t-shirt. My legs were still hairy. My brown shoulder length hair was too straight. What was I going to do? In the short ten seconds that I had to think I decided to go out and face him. What was his name again? I didn't want to meet him in the first place. Derrick and Gina were putting me up to this.

Gina panicked and said, "Girl, look at you. You look like crap! Once he sees you, he's going to run away screaming."

"Thanks."

Gina unplugged the curling iron knowing we had no time to use it. Before Gina could stop me, I walked out of the bathroom. I could hear my sister still in the bathroom using colorful profanity to express my lack of personal design. I guessed I could have let her French braid my hair or put it in a bun or something. But I felt rebellious and was fed up with looking like a Barbie doll for men. It was time they accepted me for who I was or leave me alone.

21

I also figured if he saw me at my worst and still liked me, we'd have a pretty good chance. Emotional wreck plus physical wreck would equal a messed up person, which would be me.

As I was walking down the hall, I could hear Derrick talking to his friend. He had an appealing voice. The more I listened, the more nervous I became. He sounded like a radio announcer or something. I wished I could remember his name.

Gina was gaining on me. Just as I was nearing the corner, she grabbed my right arm and yanked me back. "Here, she said as she handed me some lipstick. At least put some lipstick on."

Instead, I placed the little tube in the back pocket of my cut-offs. I was sure that she was going to hit me. We both walked into the living room to greet Mr. Friend of Derrick's. Before I could lift my eyes off the floor to see him Gina said, "Oh, look Sandy! He's vanilla just like you!"

I couldn't believe she said that! No, I take that back. I could believe it. Still, I was sure my face turned a shade of rose.

He laughed and smiled but when he looked at me, he frowned. Uh oh. He was disappointed. Derrick also frowned when he looked at me. What? They've never seen a woman au natural before? But Derrick cleared his throat and introduced me, "Jacob, this is Sandra Ray, but you may call her Sandy."

I was studying him. He was about an inch taller than me. (I was five ten.) Jacob was pretty well built with light brown hair, light brown eyes? light. Jerry had dark chocolate skin and was a big man all around. Don't get me wrong, Jerry wasn't fat, he was all muscle. Hmm, Jacob was little compared to Jerry, but I could see myself with him.

I had made it pretty obvious that I was inspecting him because he asked, "Did I pass your exam?" He smiled with perfect white teeth. It was the kind of smile that I hated. The type a guy always wore when he knew he looked good. It was the kind of smile that would eventually break my heart. "You haven't taken it yet," I snapped. Was that a bitchy thing to say? I guessed it was because Gina pinched my arm so hard I almost cried. My eyes watered. Derrick also gave me a warning glare. Okay, I'll be nice, I thought.

"So," was the only thing that came out of my mouth. I was trying to think of something nice to say or ask. "Would you like something to drink?"

"Sure. I'll have a beer if you have one."

He's an alcoholic. I felt like telling him he had just failed my test but instead I strolled into the kitchen. "Get me one too, please," Derrick said

"Me too." That was Gina of course.

I somehow managed to carry four beers from the kitchen to the living room. Derrick and Gina were sitting on the couch, and Jacob was sitting on the floor. I noticed his legs. Nice. They went well with the gray shorts he was wearing. I had an urge to bite him but of course I didn't.

Gina was laughing at something Derrick had said when I walked in. I passed each of them a Miller. "How do you like working with Derrick?" Gina asked. I sat down on the plush beige carpet. I was facing Jacob.

"He's a great person to work with. I?" blah, blah, blah? I? I? I. He kept talking about himself. I took a few gulps of beer. Soon it was almost empty. "So, what do you do?" I finally asked him before letting out a quiet belch.

Everyone turned and looked at me. They were shocked that I had spoken a few words. He smiled. I hated his smile. It was nothing compared to Jerry's smile. "I'm a pediatrician."

A pediatrician. Wow. Crap! Was I supposed to be impressed by that? I was, but that wasn't the point. "What in the world would you?" Before I could continue with my question, the doorbell rang. It was our dinner. Pizza.

While Derrick paid the delivery boy, Jacob escaped into the bathroom. "I ought to slap you upside your head," my sister threatened.

I sniffed then muttered a challenge, "Go ahead." I was pushing it and moved away from her quickly before she did something to me.

Gina was just about to get out of her seat and break every bone in my body when Derrick reentered with the pizza. "Sandy, cut the crap. He's a nice guy."

"How do you know?" I took the last gulp of my beer then continued. "It sounds like you just met the guy. He moved here? when? Six weeks ago, from Iowa. How much can you know about a person in six weeks?"

"I know he isn't married," Gina said, narrowing her eyes at me with her hands on her hips. "You were dating Jerry for two years and you didn't know he was married."

Ouch. Why did she have to throw that in my face? I felt a lump developing in my throat.

Jacob returned. His eyes were red, and he was sniffing. Hmmm? that's suspicious. Coming out of the bathroom with red eyes and sniffing. What was he doing in the bathroom? I wondered. "Would you like some pizza?" I asked.

"Mmmm. I'd love some." Gina went into the kitchen and brought out some more beer.

I usually didn't drink but considering the past few weeks; I had another beer. I quietly ate pizza and listened to the others talk. When I was on my third slice and sipping some more beer, Jacob scared me by abruptly asking, "What do you do Sandra Ray?"

"Call me Sandy."

"Sandy," he said. I wasn't sure, but I thought I detected a little annoyance in his voice as well as his expression. He wasn't sincere with his question. I could have lied and said I was a stripper just to see what he would do. I contemplated it for a minute as I took a bite of pizza and chewed. After I had swallowed, I said honestly, "I'm a salesclerk and college student." I dropped the rest of the pizza onto a napkin and took another gulp of beer.

Suddenly, I wasn't feeling too good. The beer made the pizza feel too thick in my stomach, and things looked a little wavy. I was a light weight. I felt a trickle of sweat roll down the side of my temple. I took a deep breath, inflating my stomach then slowly let the breath out. I had recently joined a Pilate's class at school with my best friend. I had found out I had been breathing in incorrectly for all the years I had lived on Earth. I also learned that the correct way of breathing can calm my nerves. I also almost passed out while I was driving once while I was doing the conscious breathing exercise. When I look back on it, it was almost an outer body experience.

Jacob must have said something to me during my conscious breathing, and I didn't hear him. He looked a little more than annoyed. "Could you two excuse us?" Jacob asked.

I thought he was talking to Gina and me. I stood up and was about to leave, but Derrick said in a commanding tone, "Sandy, stay."

My mouth opened. I was still standing. I watched Gina and Derrick leave me alone with the stranger. Jacob moved from the floor to the couch. He patted the cushion next to him signaling me to sit down. I stayed standing. "Please, sit down."

My stomach wasn't feeling too great. I sat down at the far end of the couch, far away from him. He hadn't touched his second beer. He opened it, but he hadn't taken any sips from it. "What's going on?" He asked.

"What do you mean?" I asked utterly confused. Why was he singing a Marvin Gaye song?

"Sandy," suddenly I loved the way he said my name. "Derrick told me that you've recently broken up with someone. He invited me over so we could become acquainted."

I inched closer to him. The closer I got to him, the more I realized he smelled so good, unlike Jerry. Jacob smelled like Eternity for Men. Mmmmmm.

"I would like for us to be friends. From what Derrick and Gina have told me you seem to be someone I'd love to get to know. But from what I've seen so far?"

My lips were on him before I could even think about what I was doing. He seemed interested. He had wrapped his arms around me and was kissing me back. But then suddenly he stopped and pulled away from me. I was warm.

He stood up. He shook his head as if he were confused. "What'd you do that for?"

"You smell good."

He placed a hand on his hip and the other over his mouth. "I gotta get out of here."

"Yeah, go. You'd leave anyway." He looked at me with sympathetic eyes.

I stayed on the couch. Actually, I laid down on the sofa. I didn't get a chance to see him leave because I fell asleep.

CHAPTER THREE: "More work and more school?"

I had a slight headache. I was grateful it was a Saturday until I remembered I had to go to work. Derrick and Gina had left me on the couch last night. According to the note taped on the refrigerator, they left me this morning too. They went grocery shopping without me. They were mad at me. I didn't blame them. I started to feel guilty as I was taking a shower. I ended up wondering if I had ruined any or all possibilities with Jacob.

But then what did Gina and Derrick expect? I dated and practically lived with Jerry for two years! He had been the center of my world. I thought I knew everything there was to know about him. He certainly knew everything there was to know about me. He knew about the time when I accidentally stole McDonalds. He also knew about all the family secrets and gossip. Oh, let's not forget, he certainly knew about the time I lost my virginity! He was there when that happened!

It was time for me to face it. Jerry was a jerk. The biggest idiot there ever was. Married. What a butthead!

I wondered if he had told his wife about me. Maybe she was one of those sick women who encouraged their husbands to have affairs. She probably gave him permission to screw somebody. Just don't fall in love and oh? make sure she's naïve and a virgin. If you did a virgin, you wouldn't get any diseases or anything.

Suddenly a thought occurred to me. Diseases. What if I caught something from him? I felt fine but didn't they say in health classes that for the woman most of the time there were no symptoms.

I always seemed to do my best thinking while I was in the shower instead of thinking when I was supposed to. I decided to make an appointment to see my doctor during the week. As I stepped out of the shower with water dripping from my hair, I saw a spider. It was huge! It was right next to my nylons hanging from the towel rack but on the wall. The spider was black and hairy looking, just like Jerry. Normally, I would have screamed. Instead, I picked up my black pumps and whacked the spider with the heel. I smiled from satisfaction. I stopped for a minute and realized I was getting a little demented. I took a piece of tissue paper and wiped the remains of the spider from the wall. I tossed it into the toilet and flushed. As it went down, I waved and said, "Bye Jerry."

The problem was that when I turned around and looked where I had hit the spider, there was a dent in the wall. The heel of my shoe fit perfectly there. What was I going to tell Gina and Derrick?? Nothing. Maybe they wouldn't notice. I shifted a towel that was hanging on a rack. It just barely covered up the hole.

I put gobs of gel into my hair to ensure the curls from my wet hair would remain there the rest of the day. I finally thought of looking at my watch. I had exactly thirty minutes to get to work. It would be in my best interest to leave for work at that moment.

I grabbed a bottle of Tylenol from the medicine cabinet and stuck it in my purse. I was sure I would need it.

As soon as I entered Robertson's Department Store, I heard someone call my name. "Sandy, come here."

It was Regina. She worked in the men's department. I looked at my watch, I was two minutes late. "Just a second. Let me check in." She stuck her tongue out at me as I turned to rush off to the executive office on the third floor. I was glad to see that it was empty. I quickly took out my lovely clock-in card and swiped it through the machine. Taking the escalator down to the first floor, to the men's department, I noticed they had already started putting Christmas decorations up. Couldn't we give Thanksgiving a chance? It was only one week away!"

I passed the jewelry department. I noticed a huge engagement ring was fifty percent off. With my added twenty percent discount... What a saving that would be! It figured I would see something like that today! Next, I passed the men's cologne. Mmmmm. Escape for men. Obsession for men... Eternity for men... Jacob? Guilt set in once again.

Regina was helping a customer. I waited until she handed the customer his receipt. She put on her I'm-so-happy-to-be-here smile and said, "Thank you and have a good day."

The customer grabbed his bag and left. "Hey," I said my usual greeting to her.

"Hey. Did you hear what happened to Joanne?"

"Joanne?" It took me a minute to remember who she was. She was one of the new girls who worked in the shoe department. "No, what happened?"

"She got fired. Stupid girl. That's all we needed was another one of us fired. Makin' all of us look bad. Guess why she got fired?" She didn't let me guess. "She stole a pair of shoes. Is that stupid or what? I mean if you are going to steal at least take something good. You know what I'm saying? So now how many of us are still workin' here? Hmm..." She stuck out her hand, which was perfectly manicured. Her long fake nails were painted red with blue sparkles on them. "Let's see? There's Tonya, Janet, Darlene, you and me. Five. Can you believe that? But then again, you are so light skinned, and you live in Simi Valley of all places. You don't count." She laughed with her hand on her flat stomach. She thought she was so funny.

I wanted to hit her. I knew she was joking, but I was sick of the Simi Valley jokes and the vanilla jokes. So, what I was an extremely light skinned Black woman and yes there were a lot of Caucasian's out there that were a lot darker than I was but really? does it matter? Should it?

29

"Sorry, I gotta go to my department now. I'm sure Laura is waiting for me."

"Okay, see you later." She was still giggling from her bad joke.

My department was on the second-floor, way in the back, where no one could see: the dresses and coats department, the often forgotten department. "Hi, Sandy. How are you?"

"Blah, but we won't talk about it right now," I said as I placed my purse in a tiny cabinet underneath the cash register.

"Okay." That was Laura. She agreed to anything and everything I said. I hated that.

I locked the cabinet and dropped the key in my skirt pocket. I was ready to begin my work day. Thankfully, it went by in a blur. At eight o'clock that evening, the announcement came over the intercom that the store was closing. By eight fifteen I was out of there.

Sunday morning, I had an urge to do something I hadn't done in a long time. It was something I hadn't done in nearly three years except Christmas and Easter. I decided it was time for me to go to church.

Yes, I woke up, dressed, ate some toast and drank some orange juice. I brushed my teeth then rushed off to church. The parking lot was full, so I had to park on the street and walk nearly half a block. As it turned out, I was half an hour late. I didn't know they had changed the schedule, I wondered when that happened. I also noticed that there was a new priest. He must have come sometime after Easter. I felt really out of place when I entered the church. It had something to do with everyone turning to look at me when the door accidentally slammed shut as I entered. I also remembered that I accidentally committed adultery. Suddenly, I felt as if I were wearing a huge neon sign above my head that was flashing the word, "Sinner" over and over again. I left while communion was being served. The door slammed again.

When I came back home, I found Gina in the laundry room. She was stuffing an enormous pile of clothes into the washer. She didn't look at me when she said, "You received three messages." I guessed she was mad at me for the way I treated Jacob.

"From yesterday or today?"

"Both," she finished stuffing the clothes in the washer. She finally looked at me. Yep, she is still mad at me. Gina could hold a grudge for a long time

"I'm sorry for Friday night's behavior. I just wasn't ready to see anyone."

"It wasn't like he proposed to you, Sandy! He's a nice guy. All Derrick and I wanted was for you to get acquainted with someone new."

"Yeah, you wanted the two of us to like each other on the first night, go out on a few dates and get married. Well, let me tell you something? After the way I have been lied to and dumped I am not ready to go limp over some guy who thinks he's so damn good looking; who thinks he can impress me with a snappy job title; and who wants to be in control of every situation? including me. No thank you. I think I really can wait two years before I consider dating someone, especially Jacob. And I don't want to hear anything from you!" I turned to leave the laundry room.

"Jerry called once last night and once this morning. Jacob called last night too." She closed the lid to the washer.

My stomach churned. I turned around to face her. "Jerry called?"

"And Jacob." She carried a hamper filled with dry clothes and headed for the master bedroom. She left me standing alone trying to figure out why Jerry would call me. It had to be some bad news. I knew that much. He had made it very clear that he couldn't contact me unless it were

31

an emergency of some sort. I was worried. What happened to him? Did he have something important to tell me? I had to find out.

I rushed off to my room and closed the door. Just as I was about to pick up the phone, it rang. Thinking that Jerry could somehow feel me thinking about him, knowing that I was worried about him, I picked up the phone while it was still on its first ring.

"Sandy?" a familiar yet strange voice asked.

"Who's this?" I asked with a frown.

"Jacob."

What do you want? "Hi, how are you?"

"Pretty good. I was wondering if you would like to meet me for lunch this afternoon. Do you like Mexican food?"

"No," I lied.

"Is that a no to going to lunch or a no to the Mexican food?"

"Both." I was sure that Derrick had told him that Mexican was my favorite. He knew I was lying. "I'm sorry if I was rude on Friday. I also apologize if I was rude just now, but I just want a little space from all men, okay?"

I heard him sigh. It was a massively disappointed sigh. "I understand."

Sure, you do. "Well, I'll see you around."

"I'll see to that, Sandy."

Whatever. "Bye." I hung up the phone before I could hear him say goodbye. I knew I was mean. I felt sorry that it was Jacob who I was venting all my anger at but at the same time it felt good.

I would be in control over whatever happened between Jacob and me. Since I was the one in control, nothing would happen.

I immediately dialed Jerry's number. An answering machine answered. A woman's voice was the one who said the outgoing message. It had to have been his wife. I hung up. I'd keep hanging up until he answered the phone.

Throughout the day, I was busy trying to get in touch with Jerry. It was useless. Finally at nine o'clock that evening I decided to give up. If it were that important Jerry would contact me again.

The next few days had crept by slowly. Usually when my days creep by it meant some sort of explosion or drama was about to happen. The question that wandered through my mind was: where was the explosion going to take place? Home? Work? School? Or over the phone whenever Jerry decided to call me back?

It turned out to be almost all of the above. It started at school on Monday, during an hour and a half break between classes. See, I had finally told Adrian, a friend since the third grade, about Jerry. "I'm glad you broke up with him. I didn't like him." That was real news to me. It seemed that whenever we double dated, she would drool all over herself when Jerry spoke to her. "He was too? too."

"Too what?"

"Too?" She was still trying to think of something. Adrian had long silky brunette hair that had subtle waves and went all the way down to her waist. Her real hair was only up to her shoulders, but her boyfriend paid for a hairdresser in LA to give her extensions. She always wore silver hoop earrings. Most often than not she was in a pair of hip-hugging jeans and a comfortable t-shirt.

"Married," I said, finding the word for her. I let my backpack fall from my right shoulder and dropped it onto the concrete. We both took a seat on the bench that was made of cement. We liked to sit right smack in the middle of the quad. That way we could see everything and everybody.

"Exactly," Adrian answered me as she placed her backpack on her lap. She unzipped the front portion of it. She took out a bag of powdered donuts. Adrian didn't need any more powdered donuts. Ever since we left high school, she'd have a bag of powdered donuts for a snack at some point during the day. The problem was that you could tell she was eating something with a lot of fat and sugar.

"But I didn't know he was married when I was seein' him."

Adrian shook her head and said, "That doesn't matter. There was something always fishy about him."

"Yeah, Gina said he stank too."

Adrian almost choked on her donut from laughing.

We were facing the library. It was an enormous library. It was four stories high. Big. I loved the library. It had held all the books I would need to get my bachelor's degree. Just as I was gazing at the wonderful pinkish colored building, I noticed a nearly baldheaded tall guy was heading in our direction. He had an enormous grin on his face and glasses. His big goofy feet walked like a duck toward us. He was big everywhere. He puckered up his lips when he was about ten feet away. Adrian dropped her donuts and stood on top of the bench. She screeched her usual high pitched cry whenever she saw Juan. "Hola, mi novio." That was the extent of her Spanish.

They kissed. The better term would be slobbered. They slobbered all over each other. I looked at my watch. Five minutes passed, and they were still slobbering. Okay, time for me to go. I grabbed my backpack and stood up. "I'll see you guys later. I've got some studying to do."

I was half hoping they would ask me to stay or invite me to lunch. But instead, Adrian was holding onto Juan for dear life, and Juan said for Adrian, "Okay, we'll see you later."

Crap. I took a deep breath, turned and headed for that big, pinkish building that held all of those books. As if I felt like studying. As if I gave a crap about increasing my knowledge. I didn't feel like reading some lame textbook. However, I did plan on studying. Honest. Even though, I didn't feel like it; I was going to study but somehow when I reached the doors to the enormous building, I felt minuscule. It had nothing to do with the construction itself. It had everything to do with me.

I bypassed the library and headed for the parking lot. I would be missing Mr. Reynolds's Archeology class. What did that have to do with being English major anyway? And what was I going to do with a degree in English? I didn't want to teach. I majored in English because that was the only subject that caught and held my interest. I love to read and write. My writing was nothing like Toni Morrison or Maya Angelou or even Sidney Sheldon. It was just me. I wrote short stories and fantasy but never had anything published. Oh no, depression time. I was glad I had the day off from work. I was not in any mood for smiling and being friendly to pain in the butt customers.

As I said before, an explosion was just waiting to happen. Tuesday, I missed school and work. I wanted to be completely alone. I wanted no thoughts about anyone or anything. Just me. I rented three movies and bought a bunch of junk food. I didn't give a second thought about the finals coming up. I had a whole day to myself.

I was writing in my journal when the phone rang and like a dummy, I answered it. "What are you doin' home? Shouldn't you be at school?" It was Gina.

I didn't say anything. I just let out a heavy sigh that I knew she could hear.

"I bet you already called in sick to work too."

Again, I didn't say anything.

"Well," she was quiet. Finally, she said in a low tone, "You deserve the day off."

I was touched she said something like that.

"Can you make some spaghetti for dinner, and pick up some French bread and some soda?"

I put down the box of caramel popcorn. "Sure."

"Thanks. Derrick and I will be home around four o'clock. Okay?"

"Okay."

I hung up the phone. Less than a second later it rang again. I guessed it was my sister again. She probably wanted to add something to the shopping list. I picked it up. "What else do you need, Gina?"

"It's not Gina."

Oh, my? My heart rate increased. "Jerry?"

"Yes. It's Jerry." He sounded like he was mad at somebody.

"I've been trying to get in touch with you?"

"Yeah, I know. That's why I called you in the first place. I would appreciate it if you would stop leaving those messages on my machine. It's upsetting my wife."

"Messages? What messages?" I never left him any messages. I always hung up when someone else picked up the phone.

"I'm talking about the crying and begging me to come back to California messages." He had enough nerve to raise his voice at me as if I were a five-year-old.

I was getting pissed! "What are you talking about?"

"Sandra Ray, you know what I'm talking about."

"For your information I never left any messages on your machine! It must have been some other ignorant woman that fell for your behind! Whenever I called, I just hung up. I thought something was wrong with you! I thought something terrible happened to you. But now, you call me up and yell at me like I did something wrong? You're the one who cheated on your wife then cheated on me while you were cheating on your wife. I suggest you get tested for HIV. Because I sure am! Ahhh! You were my first and only! Oh! I hate you! You are such a jerk! I hope I never see you again!" I slammed the phone back onto its receiver. My face was red. I was trembling and gasping for breath. I also had saliva dripping from the side of my mouth. I wiped it away. As I did so, a tear rolled down my cheek.

I wrapped the navy terry cloth robe that had once belonged to my father tighter. But suddenly, I had to throw up.

I ran to the bathroom and knelt in front of the toilet. I hurled just in time. When I was sure I was done, I flushed the toilet then walked over to the sink. Rinsing my mouth out with water didn't seem to get rid of the taste of bile. So, I decided on some seven-up. I resumed sitting in front of my sister and brother-in-law's television with caramel popcorn in one hand, remote control on my lap and drink in my other hand.

Somewhere in my brain I began to think. When that happens, I usually discover something about myself. I started counting back the last thirty days. My period was thirty-five to forty days ago. The last time I did the horizontal mambo was sometime around then. Okay, I'm lying. The last time was a few days before he left.

I couldn't be pregnant! Just because I threw up a few caramel popcorn kernels, it doesn't mean I was with child. Could I start having morning sickness in the first month? I always thought it was two or three months later? or was that when the morning sickness wore off?

I couldn't believe I was sitting in front of the television and just casually thinking about it. Shouldn't I be in a state of panic? Gina would kill me if I were pregnant. Then she would hunt down Jerry. Something snapped inside of me. I quickly turned off the television and changed into a pair of blue jeans and a T-shirt. I didn't have any trouble getting into my blue jeans. That was a good sign, wasn't it?

I then drove my gray Honda to Adrian's house. Right now, Adrian's parents were at work. The house would be a safe place to talk about it. Of course, it could also mean that Juan was there.

I parked my car across the street from her house. Just as I thought, Juan's rinky-dinky car was parked in her driveway. I stayed in the car and stared at the two-story house with its nicely kept lawn. It surely looked like a place to call home. Adrian's mom and dad were still together. Her parents were always happy to be around each other and were always affectionate and playful. Home. I missed that sense of security. The feeling of being able to walk in or out of a place and know it will still be there. It didn't matter what I did or didn't do, but it was a place I could go and sleep and wake up and feel safe. It was all a lie, though, wasn't it? Was there any such thing as security? Real security? I started to miss my mom. But right now, I had to worry about becoming a mom. I did my best to straighten my posture. Maybe that was what being an adult meant, to have the ability to be strong and face the hard truths in life.

I contemplated whether or not I should interrupt them. A second later I decided that qualified as an emergency where strong friendship and unity was needed. I had a right to disturb them. I got out of the car and slammed the door as hard as I could. I was hoping they heard the slam. I wanted to give Juan a signal that I was coming in. Next, I walked across the street and knocked on the door. No answer. I rang the doorbell. No answer. I knocked again. No answer. I pounded on the door with both fists and hit it repeatedly like a drum? finally an answer.

"Sandy, can't it wait?" I heard Juan shout from inside. The door was still closed. He was looking through the peek hole.

"No! It can't!" I yelled as if Juan wasn't there. "Adrian, I need your help!"

I heard them arguing. I guessed they were trying to get decent but for Juan that was kind of hard. I heard Juan yell something in Spanish. "Same to you!" Adrian yelled as she opened the door. Adrian's hair was messy. The shirt she wore was hanging off of her shoulders. I was pretty sure she was in her birthday suit under the shirt. I also realized she was in one of Juan's shirts. Her breasts were sagging. I wished she could have at least put on a bra. "What's wrong Sandy?"

I stepped inside the house and folded my arms. I saw that a part of Juan's hairy butt made a dash for the stairs. I didn't want to waste anyone's time so I just said it, "I might be pregnant," I stated in a shaky panicky voice.

Adrian clasped Juan's shirt around her neck and said, "Oh my God?"

Adrian led me to the dining room table, "Did you see a doctor?"

"No. I was planning to? I just… I'm…"

"Don't worry about it. I'll get Juan to get a test from the supermarket."

I didn't want Juan to be a part of this. "Adrian, I?"

Before I could stop her, she was using her big mouth. "Juan!" She called out again, "Juan, baby?" she cleared her throat then yelled again, "Put some pants on and get down here. We need your help!"

Juan was mumbling something as he entered the dining room. "What?" he asked crankily, giving me a wicked glare. He wanted to ensure I understood his message. He did not want me here at the moment.

"I need you to pick up one of those pregnancy tests from the grocery store." Just then Juan's face turned pale, his eyebrows raised, and he pointed a finger at himself. When Adrian realized what Juan was thinking, she shook her head and said, "No, no, no? it's not for me." She managed a smile.

He let out a profound and relieved sigh. "How many do you need?"

"Just one," I said.

"No, get three just to make sure."

"Okay."

That was easy. Usually when a favor involved me, Juan would automatically say no. I guessed he was just happy it wasn't Adrian who needed the test.

"And Juan? don't tell your friends. Don't tell anyone."

He nodded in agreement with support in his eyes. He kissed Adrian on the cheek, reached in the pockets of his jeans for his car keys and was out the door. Adrian and I talked while we waited for Juan to return. I don't exactly remember what we talked about. It was just anything to keep my mind off the possibilities. Finally, after about a half an hour Juan showed up. "Man, you wouldn't believe how many tests they have to choose from. I didn't know which one to get, so I bought five of them." He dumped a brown paper bag onto the glossy black dining room table. "You should have seen the look the salesclerk gave me. She didn't even bother to say, "Have a nice day" or anything. She was a..."

Adrian gave Juan a look that told him not to finish his sentence. She stood up and kissed Juan on the cheek. "Thank you, Juan. Do you think you could go home now?"

Juan shoved his hands in his pockets and let his mouth fall open. After a moment, he closed his mouth again. His face turned red. He looked at me. Blinked. Then he looked at Adrian. "Will you call me?"

"Of course."

I bit my lower lip. I knew that Juan was upset that I ruined his good time with Adrian. I also knew he wanted to know the results of the test that I was soon to be taking. Thankfully, Adrian knew that I wanted it to be just the two of us. I stared at the paper bag that was still on the table. The contents of the bag were going to tell me my future. I was scared. I placed a hand on top of my belly. I was starting to feel bloated. There might be a baby developing right now. What was I going to do if there was?

I was twenty-three years old. I spent three and a half years at a community college and then transferred to

California State University, Northridge. I only had one year left to graduate. Thirteen months to be exact. I was going to graduate in December of next year. But if I was pregnant, what was going to happen? I mean, would the University allow a pregnant woman to attend their campus? What about work? Would I be able to work? What about Gina? Oh no. Gina! What would she do to me? She would send me back to Mom. That really would not be too bad. Right now, I needed Mama. My thoughts went back to Gina. She'd end up getting on a plane to Georgia and would do something to Jerry.

I was twenty-three years old, but I still felt like I was only sixteen. I guessed it had something to do with being so dependent on my family. But then look at Adrian, she was the same age as me, and she still lived with her parents, both parents. She didn't even work. At least I had joined the workforce. Why was I comparing myself to Adrian anyway? She wasn't the one who might be pregnant. She wasn't the one who was alone.

My mom lived in Northern California. When my parents were married, we all lived out here in Simi. In fact, we lived a block from my sister's house. It wasn't anything compared to Adrian's house. It seemed that after my sister left the house to get married everything just fell apart at home. My Dad retired and wanted to do his own thing, and Mom wanted to do her own thing. To make a long story short, they got a divorce a month after I graduated from high school. Dad moved to Nevada and Mom moved to Fresno.

I tried living with Mom for about six months. That was when I was trying to figure out what I was going to do with my life, before I started attending the community college. My mom didn't help me too much. She was busy with her newfound social life. She went out on dates almost every night. It was hard for me to live with her. I was home more than she was. When Gina told me I could stay with her, I eagerly caught the next Greyhound and moved in.

The slamming of the Adrian's front door brought me back. I hadn't noticed Juan walked out of the house. Adrian had walked him out. She was the one who slammed the door. "You know I love Juan, right? But sometimes he gets on my nerves."

I didn't say anything. I guessed it was because I didn't have anything to say. I was too worried. Adrian sat next to me and turned the paper bag upside down. Five boxes stumbled out of the bag. We each grabbed a box. While I was reading the back of the carton, my stomach started to ache. It must have been my nerves or something. I continued to read the box. "I have to wait until the first-morning urine to take this one. What about that one?"

"Same thing. You have to use your first-morning urine."

I made a face. "Why don't you just say pee? I hate that word? urine," I shivered.

"What's wrong with urine? It sounds better than pee or piss."

I narrowed my eyes and crinkled my nose, "Don't say that!"

"You know, Sandy, you can be immature sometimes. It is clear that you've had sex before, but I bet you haven't even said the word penis."

I made another face. She was right. I never could say that word. Even when Jerry tried to talk to me about sex, I could say almost anything, but I couldn't say 'penis.'"

"Go Ahead. Say it, Sandy. It's liberating, and it will be good therapy for you. Go ahead. Say it." Adrian had determination written on her face.

She was asking too much from me. "Can we please just take care of my situation?"

"Not until you say it," she said with her arms wrapped around the tests that were still sitting on the dining room

42

table. My stomach started hurting again. It felt like cramps. I slouched over for a minute and waited for it to subside. I felt like I had to go to the bathroom.

As soon as I was able to stand up, I felt something. It was something that I very much welcomed. "Adrian, do you have any pads?"

"Pads?" She looked up at me. When she finally understood what I was asking she jumped out of her seat. She gave me a big hug and was cheering me on. "It started! It started! It started! Thank goodness." She was happier than I was.

"Adrian, I need a pad now." While she was hugging me, my pants were getting stained. She rushed off to her room and returned carrying a super pad with wings, along with a sweatshirt to wrap around my waist. "Here you go," she said with a smile. When I came out of the bathroom, I glanced at my watch. It was already two thirty. I had to get back home. I still had to fix dinner and clean up the house. It was pretty much a disaster when I left it. Derrick was a neat freak, a real fanatic. My sister told me that whenever he took a crap, he would take a shower right afterward.

I felt empty inside. The realization once again that I was alone set deep inside of me. Sure, I had my sister and friends but when it came down to it, I was alone.

"Sandy, what is your problem?" Adrian asked angrily and annoyed.

"Nothing," I said then took a deep breath. I grabbed my keys from the table and looked around for my purse. I suddenly realized that I had forgotten my purse, which meant I had been driving around without a license. All I needed now was to get pulled over and not have my license.

Adrian noticed that I had picked up my keys and was heading for the door. "Oh, okay, I see where you're at. You come over pounding on my door like a mad woman. Scare me half to death by telling me you were pregnant and when you find out you aren't, you wanna just up and leave?" She placed her hands on her hips and shook her long fake brunette hair.

"Yeah. It's terrible, isn't it? You can do the same to me. But I gotta go," I gave her a hug and was on my way.

I drove very carefully. I made sure I was doing the speed limit and was cautious of every single swerve and curve I took. But the speed limit was just too slow! When I finally got home, it was almost three o'clock.

The house was a mess. How could one person make such a mess? Bits of caramel popcorn were all over the couch and rug. Three empty seven-up cans were on the table. DVD cases were on the floor in front of the television. The blanket was hanging off of the couch. The remote control was on the ground.

That was nothing compared to the kitchen. I still had the unused portion of pancake batter sitting in the missing bowl, not only that but also some of the batter? okay, a lot of the batter? had spilled on the countertop and the stove. When it happened, I didn't care. So now it was almost caked on the counter top and stove. But who was I kidding it was now a part of the counter top and stove.

So basically, for the next forty minutes I was running all over the house scrubbing, rubbing, picking and spraying. Yep. I sprayed potpourri stuff in the air and made it smell like peaches all over the house. The problem was I sprayed too much and started to feel lightheaded. I had to open some windows. In my efforts to open one of the windows, I broke a nail. But I was rushing around so much that I didn't have a chance to complain. I got a work out from cleaning up the place because I had started to perspire. I had been breathing heavy and hadn't realized it until I finally took a seat for a moment. I felt a little lightheaded; I guessed it was because I was on my period? Thank goodness.

I remembered I still needed to go to the store to get stuff for dinner. So, I made a quick drive to the grocery store and planned to make a quick trip back. The problem was that during my quick trip back home, a motorcycle officer pulled me over. I was just one block away from home. I didn't realize I was doing fifty-five in a forty-mile zone. Then when I saw him flashing his blue and red lights, I thought it was for the car in front of me. That guy was going a lot faster than I was. But just to make sure I pulled over anyway. The officer parked his motorcycle right behind me.

I watched him through my rearview mirror as he climbed off the bike. I was mesmerized as his thigh muscles stretched in his form-fitting tan pants. Then he turned around for a second. I guessed he was reaching for his pad and pen. His butt was solid and round. Mmmm… Mmmmm.

What I needed to know was why did someone who was about to give me a ticket have to have a body like his? He walked over to my side of the car. As he did so, he had his arms to the side. Only his arms didn't touch his side. They just hung because he was too buff for them to reach his side. His waist was so small.

I took a deep breath and rolled down my window. I wanted to say something brilliant. I wanted to give him a real reason I was speeding.

"License and registration please," he said before any words could come out of my mouth.

Dang, couldn't he at least make eye contact? Aren't police officers supposed to have People skills? Geesh, I was more than a person who just broke the law by speeding. I was a woman.

I reached over to my glove compartment and pulled out my proof of registration.

I looked through my purse and found my license. I was glad I had my purse with me. I handed both items to him.

He was writing on his little pad. I studied him as if I were studying an exquisite art piece. I wanted to remember this guy: blond hair, green eyes, dimples and full lips.

"Mam, do you know how fast you were going?"

"I? I"

He finally looked at me, but it was with a scowl on his face. "You were going fifty-seven miles per hour in a forty-mile zone. Have you been to traffic school in the past eighteen months?"

"I? no."

"You're lucky then. This ticket won't show up on your record if you go." He handed me back my license and registration. "Sign here please." I signed it and then he gave me the damn ticket "Here you go and be sure to have a beautiful day." He smiled. He had the worst teeth I ever saw! They were yellow, crooked and bunched together. It ruined the rest of his appearance.

He climbed back onto his motorcycle and waited for me to start my car again. I thought he would leave once I started the ignition but nope, he waited for me to get going. That S.O.B. followed me home. Then he had enough nerve to wave at me when I got out of the car.

I carried the bag of groceries in one hand and the ticket in the other. Just my luck, I found Derrick and Gina's car in the driveway. I barely reached the door when Derrick swung the door open. He was huffing and puffing with overt anger. It appeared he was angry with me. I gritted my teeth as I waited to find out why. "Why did you leave the windows open in the house?" Crap. Crap, crap, crap.

He didn't even ask me if I needed help carrying the bag. "This is Simi Valley, Derrick. We can leave the house for a couple of minutes with the windows open." We really couldn't but I tried to lie, anyway.

"Not in my house. The next time you decide to leave I want you to lock up. Got it!" He followed me into the house. Didn't I say he could be so serious? He didn't know how to relax.

Then Gina jumped in "Girl, didn't I ask you to have dinner made and ready when I got home? What were you doing?"

Was I their maid? Did miss something when I decided to move into their house? There had to be a mix up somewhere because Gina was not my mother and Derrick was most definitely not my father. They both stood in the kitchen with their hands on their hips. They were both silent, and both were staring at me.

I broke the silence by stating, "I have just had an awful day. I didn't even have to go to school or work to have it. I was just… I went to the store for few minutes to pick up the spaghetti mix and stuff." I put the bag on the counter and explained, not that I had to explain but continued anyway, "Because I was in such a rush to fix dinner, guess what I got?"

"What?" They both asked in cranky unison.

I dangled the ticket between my thumb and index finger. Derrick snatched it away from me while Gina started laughing. Derrick began to complain as if he was the one who got the ticket, and then Gina grabbed it from him.

I started to take out the groceries, but Gina's hyena laughter stopped me. Derrick escaped into their bedroom. Gina was still standing in the middle of the kitchen laughing. When my sister laughed a real laugh, she tended to get loud, really loud. She started stomping her feet. She wanted the whole world to know she was laughing.

I was getting just slightly perturbed by her amusement. I couldn't understand why she was laughing so hard. It wasn't that funny. In fact, it wasn't funny at all. Finally with a frown I asked her, "Gina, what is so funny? You just got a ticket last month. I didn't laugh at you."

She calmed down a little bit. She stopped stomping her feet and sat down at the table. She giggled a little more then wiped the tears from her eyes. "Yeah, but at least they didn't say I was white." She started her uproar again. What was she talking about? I frowned. She somehow managed to hand me the ticket and said, "Look." She pointed to a spot on the ticket. There was a column, which indicated the race or nationality of the offender. The police officer checked off the box that read, "white."

"I don't believe this?"

Gina bent over and stomped her foot on the ground. Each time she stomped her foot the chair would scoot back a little bit. I wanted to grab one of the tight braids and yank it out of her hair.

CHAPTER FOUR: "My good reputation gone bad?"

Considering the day I had on Tuesday, I decided to be a good girl for the rest of the week. I didn't play hooky from either school or work.

Friday finally arrived. I was sitting in my last class for the week, Study of Poetry. I would have enjoyed the class very much if I liked poetry. A lot of people are under the false assumption that just because I was an English major I have a passion or love for poetry. I could not stand it.

Dr. Raymond was busy lecturing on a poem that I was supposed to have read on Monday but didn't. It was the "Goblin Market" by Christina Rossetti. I had my pen and paper out I was writing down almost everything the professor said I knew that I would never get around to reading it. For the final I would just memorize my notes and write down everything Dr. Raymond said. I'd most likely get a 'C' in the class.

After class, Tim James balled up a piece of paper and threw it at my head. I saw it coming from the corner of my eye and ducked just in time. He was one of Juan's jerky friends. Every once in a while, I had to put up with him, mostly at parties or something. The funny thing was that he was in almost all of my English classes, but we rarely spoke to one another. We had a mutual dislike for one another.

His red head and freckled face appeared right in front of me as I stood up. My backpack was hanging from my right shoulder. "Did you get the results from the test?"

"Test? What test?" I was worried and asked in a panic, "Did we have a test on Tuesday? I was absent."

His green eyes looked down on me. He smiled a little. "I'm not talking about school, Sandy." He chewed on his lower lip a little. I thought he was going to bite down on it, but he licked it instead.

"Then what test are you talking about?" I moved away from him. I walked toward the door.

We were both in the hall and surrounded by other students. He said, "The test Juan had to get for you."

I stopped right where I was. Someone almost rammed right into me. I couldn't believe that Juan told anyone, especially Tim. But Tim was one of Juan's best friends. It hurt, though because Juan knew that I didn't like Tim.

I raised my head and looked up at him. I crossed my arms and said, "That is none of your business, Tim."

He blushed but said, "Look, Sandy. I know we aren't exactly close or anything, but still? I'm concerned."

I felt a sudden feeling of anger. It wasn't concern that Tim felt. I knew him too well. He was just looking for something to gossip about. He was one of the biggest gossipers on campus. He loved getting into other people's business. He should have been journalism major instead.

I glanced down at my watch. "I have to go. I've got to work tonight."

He looked hurt that I was leaving him. "Adrian and Juan are going to the movies tonight. Would you want to tag along?"

I tried hard not to roll my eyes. Why was he pretending to be interested in me all of the sudden? He used to go out of his way to irritate me or pick on me. I took a deep breath, cleared my throat and said, "No. As I said, I have to work." I headed for the stairs. I hoped Tim would remain behind, but I found him a few seconds later walking right beside me. He was quiet. We walked down the two flights of stairs.

When we finally made it outside, he said, "Sandy, you don't like me very much, do you?"

"Are you sure you want me to answer that?" I asked as I kept walking, accelerating my pace a bit more with each step, hoping he'd get the message.

"You're right. I don't want to know."

"I'll see you on Monday." I dismissed him with a wave. As I did so, I reminded myself of Gina.

"Laura, can I ask you something?"

"Sure," I knew she was going to say that.

She strolled over to where I was. I had my elbows on the counter next to the register. She stood right behind the register and looked at me. "Why is it that I can't go through an ordeal without the whole world knowing about it?"

She tilted her head. Her auburn hair moved along with her head. "Are you talking about your pregnancy?"

I stood up straight rather quickly at her remark. How in the world did she hear about that? I looked at her. "Laura, I'm not pregnant. Who told you that?"

"Regina, from the men's department. She said that Rachel from cosmetics friend had told her at school and then?"

"Nevermind," I put my hands up to stop her from giving the rest of the gossip trail. I tilted my head from side to side cracking my neck to ease the tension. It felt good that I smiled a little as I said, "Just tell Regina that I am not pregnant. That should take care of everyone else." I knew it had to be Tim James fault. He was one other reason I couldn't trust men.

"To answer your question, I think people just get bored with their lives, so they have to hear about others. That's why soap operas are so hot. People need to see other people's pains make their lives seem a lot better. But I'm glad to hear that you aren't pregnant."

"Thanks."

She walked away from me and went into the fitting room. I didn't know why she went in there. We only had one customer the entire evening, and she had left an hour ago. I glanced at my watch. I only had an hour, and a half left before the store closed.

Suddenly I felt like someone was watching me. I knew it had to be security. I glanced at the manikin that was near a register. It was one of the Security manikins. The eyes had cameras in them. Ingenious, huh? I walked away from the register and stood right in front of the doll. I looked straight into the manikin's eyes and flipped it off while laughing an exaggerated psychotic laugh. Less than a second later the phone rang. I rushed back over to the register and answered the phone while it was still on its first ring.

"Evening wear. This is Sandy speaking. How may I help you?"

"Sandy, get to work and don't flip me off again or I will have to report you."

"Kevin? Hi, how are you?" I smiled right at the manikin. Kevin was one of my buddies. He was the only person from Security I liked.

"I am tired, and I want to go home. But Sandy, you were just lucky it was me and not Mr. Jones." Mr. Jones was the store manager.

I rolled my eyes and said, "I knew it was you. Laura told me earlier that Mr. Jones wasn't here today."

"What are you doing tonight?" He breathed heavily and said, "You look beautiful. Do you want to go out? Dancing or something?"

That sounded like fun, but I was tired. "Thanks for asking but I just want to go home tonight."

"Okay, I'll talk to you later." He could have asked me one more time. He gave up too easily.

Later when I was leaving the store, I changed my mind. Kevin was sitting in his usual spot at closing time. He was sitting on a cheap folding chair right smack in front of the Lower Level Exit doors in the Men's Department. He had his arms crossed and was leaning back in his chair. It was his duty to check all of the employee's purses and bags, making sure no one took anything they weren't supposed to.

When it was my turn to be checked, he said, "Spread em. Empty all your pockets."

I gently slapped the back of his head. "Ouch." He rubbed the spot where I had hit him.

I opened my purse. He looked inside. It pissed me off. He should have known me by now. He should have known that I would never steal anything. But I guessed in his work he probably couldn't trust anyone no matter how long he knew them.

I was about to close my purse, but Kevin stuck his hand in my bag and pulled out a pack of my cinnamon gum. "Boy, I don't think so." I put my hands on my hips and tapped my foot. "You'd better stick that right back where you got it."

"Come on Sandy. Geesh, I need something to chew on. I'm hungry."

My mouth twisted to one side as I contemplated. "Okay. Go ahead. But don't reach in my purse like that anymore. You might find something you aren't supposed to."

He ignored my comment and asked, "Are you sure you don't want to go out?"

"No," I smiled. "You want to go out to eat and do whatever afterward?"

"Oooooh," he uncrossed his arms then sat up straight. His shiny brown hair fell across his shoulders. He had beautiful hair. It almost reached the middle of his back. "Are you saying we can do a little bit of sinning after dinner?"

I tilted my head to the side and made a face. I didn't have to answer him. He got the message. He held up his hands in defense and said, "Okay, okay. I won't push it." Then he mumbled under his breath, "Asked her out almost every night for the past year?"

I didn't think he planned for me to hear that. But I suddenly realized he was right. He had asked me out almost every Friday, but I never went out with him. I wondered why I never went out with him. Then it hit me? Jerry? the butthead. I was faithful, always true to Jerry.

"How much longer are you going to be?" I asked.

"Not too much longer. I have to wait for Rick to come, and I have?"

"I tell you what," I accidentally interrupted him. "I'll just pick up some hamburgers and fries down the street and come back. By that time, you should be ready, and we can just eat it here or in the parking lot."

"Now that's original," he grinned. "Sounds good."

I was on my way. I went to McDonald's about two blocks from the store. I didn't feel like getting out of the car, so I went through the drive-thru. I ordered two Big Mac's, two large fries, and two large sodas. Kevin was sitting in his car when I finally made it back. I parked right next to his car. Kevin got out of his car and strolled over to mine. He opened the door for me as soon as I unlocked it. He stuck his hands out. I passed him the bags of food. As I climbed out of the car, I realized how nice it was outside. It was just the right temperature. There was a little breeze blowing.

We decided to sit on the hood of his car. I didn't care that I had a skirt on. I took my pumps off and placed them next to me.

We gobbled the hamburgers down rather quickly. We were both hungry. But when we got to the fries, we slowed down. While we were eating, we gossiped about everyone, and anything associated with Robertson's Department

Store. He told me about the different employees he caught stealing money out of the registers and taking merchandise. He said that most of the people that were arrested were employees. I was shocked. Now I understood why he checked my purse all the time. "It must be hard for you to trust anyone."

"No, not really."

I tilted my head to the side to look at him.

"Yeah, you're right," he admitted. He stuffed the last of his French fries in his mouth and swallowed. He wiped his hands on a napkin. "You want the rest of my fries?" I offered, holding my stomach. I was stuffed.

"Sure," he accepted them easily. "So how is everything for you outside of Robertson's?"

I made a face, "Fonky."

It appeared he didn't understand what I meant by fonky. So, I explained, "Things have been pretty bad for me lately."

"Is that why you decided to go out with me tonight?"

"Yes and no." I took a sip of my soda. I leaned back on his windshield and stared up at the stars. "I just needed to do something else other than go home. It's not even home. It's my sister and brother in laws house."

"So, I am just something else to do on a Friday night?" he asked as he also leaned against the windshield.

I realized that I probably hurt his feelings. "Kevin, I didn't mean to say? Umm… I… I just…"

"You just broke up with your boyfriend, right?

"Yes, exactly." I glanced away from the constellation Cassiopeia to look at Kevin.

"I thought so."

We were both quiet for a while. Finally, Kevin said, "You know Sandy, I usually don't listen to rumors. But I heard one today that you are pregnant. Is it true?"

Instead of answering his question, I asked, "What if it were true?" I wanted to know the answer.

"Well, I for one, certainly don't have any right to judge you one way or the other?"

I shook my head in disagreement. He was going to continue saying something, but I interrupted him. "You have a right to judge me just as much as anyone else. We've worked together for a long time. How would you feel if I were pregnant? Be honest."

We continued to look at each other. "I don't know how to answer that. I hardly know you outside of Robertson's."

"I guess that wasn't a fair question. Sorry. I am just so tired of people asking me if I'm pregnant. I don't know what I would have done if I were. Jerry ended up being married and moved to the other side of the country. I guess I would have moved in with my mom or something."

"You mean, all this time you were seeing a married man?"

He didn't seem to be judging me the way Gina had. He was merely asking me a valid question. So, I answered it. I told him everything. I even told him about Jacob. When I was through, he said, "I can see the best thing you need right now is a buddy."

It didn't sound corny to me. It just seemed honest. I took a deep breath then said, "Yep." I let out a sigh.

"So, tell me what goes on outside Robertson's for you, Kevin."

"When I am not working, I'm at school."

That wasn't telling me much. I suddenly wondered if this was how Jacob felt? left out if in the cold. So, I decided to dig. "There's more to your life than that?"

"Yeah, you're right. I just never have time to do the things I'd like to be doing."

"Like?"

"Camping, ride my motorcycle?" He seemed to be thinking of other stuff he'd like to do. "Read a good book. You know? Not one for school or because I have to. Just sit back somewhere quiet and read."

I laughed. He gently pushed me on the shoulder. "I never pictured you as the nerdy type. Mr. Cool Security Guy with the hot butt and impressive forearms."

He laughed too.

We were quiet for some time. We were just sitting on the hood of his car and staring up at the stars. It was nice. I almost fell asleep because it was so nice. I hadn't realized that my head was resting on his left shoulder until he said, "Sandy, this is nice, but it's getting late."

I glanced at my watch. He was right. It was almost eleven thirty. He gathered the trash, and I slipped my shoes back on. We climbed off his hood. I wasn't sure how I should say goodbye to him. It wasn't a date or anything. I wasn't about to kiss him. I didn't know if I should just wave to him or what.

I reached inside my purse and took out my keys. While he dumped the trash, I opened my car door. I heard him holler, "Sandy, wait up!"

I stood with the car door open. His hair flapped as he jogged towards me. "I need a hug." Me too. We embraced each other. It felt good. He was such a strong guy, but he gave such gentle, warming hugs. I wanted to stay in his arms for a while. But finally, he let me go. "I'll see you later."

"Okay," was the only word that managed to come out of my mouth.

CHAPTER FIVE: "Hey, we're family?"

Somewhere I could hear somebody calling my name. I heard it again. It was a whining, whispering sound. Then I smelled bacon. My stomach reacted to the scent. I heard my name again. This time it was clear. "Sandy!" It was my sister. She was in my room.

I opened one eye. "What?" I asked in a groggy voice.

"Breakfast is almost ready. Get up."

"Just stick mine in the oven. I'll be up in an hour."

Gina yanked the covers off my bed. I knew she was going to do that. She always did whenever she wanted me to get out of bed, ever since we were kids. Both of my eyes unwillingly opened. "What's the special occasion?" I asked with a frown and a yawn.

"Nothing unusual. I just wanted the family together for breakfast."

"Family? What family?" I sat up and scratched my frizzy head. My pinky got stuck for a brief moment until I yanked it out. A small amount of hair came out.

Gina was already in jeans and a peach sweatshirt. She put her hands on her hips and said, "What do you mean what family? I'm talking about Derrick, you and me!"

I let out another good yawn and stretched. My whole entire body felt the stretch and my lungs filled with air. I felt pretty good this morning and smiled.

Gina caught my smile. "What's that about? You came home late last night. What did you do?"

"Nothing." I slipped on my pink furry slippers.

"Then why are you still smiling?"

I finally stood up and explained, "I just had dinner with a friend from work." I left Gina standing in my doorway. My stomach couldn't wait any longer. It wanted the French toast, and the bacon smelled so good.

As I was walking down the hall, I could feel my sister's presence right behind me. "Hmm? was it a guy friend?"

"Yeah," I said smiling.

We finally reached the kitchen. Derrick had his back facing us. He was looking for something in the refrigerator. I was standing right behind him when he turned around. He let out a little yelp and almost dropped a carton of orange juice. "Sandy!" He placed his left hand over his heart. "You scared the crap out of me!"

Gina and I laughed a little.

"It's not funny." He poured himself a glass of juice. "Sandy brush your hair? and please, brush your teeth."

"Why?" I was reaching up into one of the top cabinets for a plate. "Gina said we're family. I don't have to brush?"

Gina interrupted my speech by bringing up the earlier subject. "Who did you go out with?"

"You don't know him. He's one of the security officers."

"Not that guy with the long hair?"

I placed a few pieces of French toast on my plate. "As a matter of fact, it was him. I had a nice time with him, too."

"I don't believe it?"

I bit into one of the two pieces of bacon on my plate. "What about Jacob, Sandy?" Derrick asked.

"What about him?" I took my seat at the black lacquer table.

Soon Derrick and Gina followed me to the table. Derrick placed a small glass of orange juice in front of me. I took a sip. I tasted the cold, pulpy, sweet yet bitter liquid as it passed my taste buds and then trickled down my throat. Mmmm. It felt and tasted so good.

"Isn't he a white guy with long girly hair?" Gina asked.

"Yeah, so?"

"What do you mean by what about him?" Derrick asked.

59

These two were getting on my nerves. "I'm not dating Jacob, and I never will." I poured syrup on my toast.

Gina let out one of her pig snorts. I smirked and narrowed my eyes at her. She rolled her brown eyes back at me. Finally, I flipped her off.

"Hey, hey?" Derrick stretched out his arms. "Stop fighting you two. I don't want to have this at my table!"

"Excuse me, but half of this table and house is mine. If I want to fight, I can fight. She's my sister! I have every right to fight with her if I want to."

"And I pay you two rent so don't try to act like you guys are my parents," I said moving my head from side to side while holding a fork with a piece of French toast on it. "And don't try to intimidate me just because you own this house. And if I want to go out with a guy, I can go out with him. Just because he's white," my eyes opened wide, "it's not going to stop me."

Gina looked at Derrick. Derrick looked down at his plate and began to saw through the four pieces of French toast. "You're right. We aren't your parents. We just want to help you. We know you've been through an awful time with your parents' divorce. And Jerry didn't help much?"

I finally chewed on the toast. Cinnamon, sugar, syrup and toast tasted so good in the morning! I closed my eyes to savor the taste.

"You aren't even listening to me, are you?" Derrick asked.

I opened my eyes to see my sister leaning back in her chair, and Derrick had both of his fists on the table. "I am listening."

"Good. I just have one thing left to say. You better think twice before you date a white guy."

"Why?" I asked him.

"Because," Gina answered for him, "you are already so light. If you go out with a white man, people are going to say that you are trying to be white. Or that you're attempting to pass or something."

"I don't care what people say."

"Maybe that's your problem," Derrick said.

I wasn't sure what he meant by that. I didn't want to know. Was he saying that I was self-centered or something? If he were, I could tell him a few things about himself that I was sure he'd be shocked to find out.

"Derrick, I know my sister more than anyone. She's stubborn. If we keep telling her not to go out with this guy, it's only going to make her want to go out with him more. The more we try to convince her that Jacob is a good man for her, the farther away she will make herself available to the possibility."

Gina was right. We all knew she was right. I was silent for a while. I refused to let the two of them ruin the breakfast they had fixed for me. When I was on my last piece of toast, I said, "You two shouldn't be so upset. I'm not dating Kevin or anything. We're just good friends. But I am letting you know now, if I do decide to date him, I will." I left the two of them at the table. I made the short journey to my bedroom and plopped down on my bed. I didn't feel the same way that I had when I first woke up. When I woke up, I felt happy. But now I felt frustrated and confused. I despised both feelings. I lay down and stared at the lumps on my ceiling.

I could understand only slightly why they thought I shouldn't date a white man. I knew that if I dated Kevin people would start to talk, especially at work. Almost sixty percent of the people I worked with also attended my school. So, I'd have to face it. My life would be very different. If not, my reputation would be different. Wait, I didn't have a reputation, at least I didn't think I did. But then again, people were probably calling me a slut or something because of the whole non-pregnancy thing.

But still, what was so wrong with a Black person dating a White person or any other race for that matter? I mean look at my family. I was light, but I had some cousins who were lighter than I was. So that had to mean that somewhere in my family tree there was someone who was white.

Then I started thinking about the cousins that were lighter than me. I recalled that they were trying to pass off as white. They didn't associate with anyone dark in the family.

It was aggravating! That wasn't what I was doing! If I started dating Kevin, it wouldn't be because I wanted to be white or anything. It would be because I liked him. Shouldn't that be the reason people dated each other? Or was that my naïve way of thinking?

Now that I was thinking about the racial and skin color issue, I thought of Jerry. He had always wanted me to get as much sun as possible. He didn't want to be seen with such a light Black girl. I had never really cared when I was dating him. I just did whatever he told me to do. I just wanted to please him. But now that I thought about it, it made me angry.

Jerry had asked me to prove to everyone around us that I was black. Why couldn't he accept my skin color for what it was? Why should I have to change my skin color? Why should I have to prove to anyone that I was black?

Suddenly I remembered an incident when I first moved to Simi. A next door neighbor had invited my sister and me to swim at her house. We were both excited by the invitation. Nancy, the little girl that invited us, was the same age as me. She had long blond hair and blue eyes. While we were swimming, she asked me if Gina was my sister. I had said, "Of course." She then asked me if I was sure. I insisted that I was. I asked her why she asked the question, and she told me because we didn't look anything alike.

I finally understood what she was saying. She was saying that my sister was dark, and I was light. Or rather that my sister was black, and I was white. So, in her eyes there was no possible way that we could be sisters. I realized not for the first time that I had an identity problem. Or I wasn't the one who had a problem identifying me, but other people had problems identifying me. I knew that I was black, but when I looked in the mirror, I saw white. I knew that when other people looked at me, they probably saw the same thing. What was it that had attracted me to Jerry in the first place? It wasn't his personality. If I had noticed his personality, I would have noticed what a jerk he was. What attracted me to him were his looks. He had dark chocolate skin. He was tall and muscular. His eyes were a dark brown. He had full lips. Maybe one of the reasons I had dated him was because he was so dark. Maybe I thought that by dating him people would see that I was black.

So, I was just as bad as Jerry. While he was using me for sex, I was using him for his blackness. The thought left me lying in my room with my eyes fixated on the ceiling for nearly an hour.

Derrick and Gina had left me to go to a matinee. I was sitting on their couch flipping through a magazine when the doorbell rang. I didn't feel like getting up. Maybe they would go away. Ding-dong. I groaned as I was forced to get my body to the door. I looked through the peek hole to see a pregnant woman with short hair. She looked familiar. Oh, I remembered. She was the neighbor from across the street.

I glanced down at myself to see if I was presentable. I guessed blue jeans and a sweatshirt were okay. My hair was pushed back with the aid of a headband. I opened the door. "Hi," I put on one of my Robertson's employee smiles. "You just moved in across the street, right?"

"Yes," she answered in a little girl's voice. "I hate to bother you, but I just wanted to introduce myself. I'm Natasha Campbell. Everyone calls me Tasha for short." She seemed to be rather nervous.

Did she come over here just to introduce herself or was there something else to it? Just then she narrowed her eyes and held her stomach. "Are you alright?"

She made a funny face. "Actually, no. I've been having labor pains for quite some time."

Labor pains? Uh oh. My brain fought hard not to switch into panic mode. Why was she not at the hospital? "Would you like me to get your husband?"

She almost started to cry. "No. We had a big fight last night. He took the kids with him to his mother's house."

What kind of husband would leave his pregnant wife alone like that? "How far apart are the pains?" That was the only question I could think of. It was always a question I heard in the movies.

"About six minutes."

I nodded and said, "Okay." I had no idea what that meant. Six minutes? Wasn't that close? I didn't know. I didn't know this woman either. What was I supposed to do? What would Gina do? I balled up my right hand into a fist and knocked it against my head a few times. Suddenly, Tasha grabbed my arm and squeezed it hard. I winced from the pain. Hospital. Get her to the hospital.

"I'll take you to the hospital. Let me get my keys." Her water better not break in my car.

I had a meaningless, one-sided conversation with Tasha while I drove to the hospital. The nurses on the second floor took care of everything and then asked me if I wanted to go into the delivery room. I didn't know what to do. I didn't know this woman, but I didn't want her to be left alone either. Maybe I should call her husband or something. But the nurse told me that she had already contacted him, and he would be here soon. So, I guessed I could probably go home. But yet I felt like I had to stay at least until he showed up.

Instead of going into the delivery room I waited in the lounge. They had a television there, so I watched cartoons and then I Love Lucy. My stomach began to growl. I could take a hint.

I decided to go down to the cafeteria. As I walked to the elevator, I had a weird unexplainable feeling. I guessed the best way to describe it would be to say I felt like something bad was about to happen. I didn't know why I had this feeling or what it meant, but I had it.

When the elevator stopped on the third floor, I understood. I was reminded that my sister, Derrick and worst of all, Jacob, worked here at the hospital. The doors slid open and there before me stood the three whom I was just thinking of. They hadn't yet realized the elevator doors opened.

"Ask her out one more time, please. I don't want my sister to date a?" Gina was saying before she turned her head and realized that elevator door opened. It was obvious she was talking about me. From the way Derrick and Gina were dressed, it appeared that they had made a special trip to see Jacob. Jacob was the only one in uniform.

I uncrossed my arms and also took a few steps forward.

"Sandy, it's so nice?" He didn't have a chance to finish his greeting because I pressed the button to close the elevator door.

I didn't feel like being bothered, especially by Jacob. Finally, the elevator arrived on the first floor. I turned to the right and passed the gift shop.

The cafeteria had about five people in it. There was a serving area. It looked like they were serving tuna sandwiches with Jello and something else, but I couldn't tell what it was. I noticed there were two vending machines in a corner. I strolled over to one. I reached into my purse and pulled out my wallet. Then I saw they wanted a dollar for a candy bar. I grumbled out loud, "Two dollars for a candy bar! I don't think so!" I looked at the other machine. "Two twenty-five for a damn soda! Shi..."

"I'll be more than happy to treat you to lunch, Sandy."

Oh, flyin' frickin frack and crap! I groaned, frowned and turned to face Jacob. "What?" I had a hunger headache, and now I had a Jacob headache.

"I'd like to have lunch with you." He had his white coat open. Underneath the jacket, he was wearing navy blue slacks and a white dress shirt. Crap, he looked so handsome. More than the first time I saw him. His light brown eyes held kind of an excitement in them. It was hard for me to breathe for a moment.

I cleared my throat then said, "It's okay. I'm not hungry." I felt like I was going to faint because I was so hungry. I had thought the French toast would last at least half the day, but it didn't.

He looked up at me, clenched his teeth then grabbed my elbow.

"Sandy, I am just asking you to have lunch with me. I'm not asking for a date, marriage, and children."

"I said I'm not hungry." I pushed his hand away from me as if it were a slimy bug.

"Why don't you like me? Or is it me? Or do you just hate all men?"

I tilted my head to the right as I put my right hand on my hip and explained, "No, I don't hate all men. I explained it all to you before on the phone. Didn't I tell you that I didn't want to be bothered? Didn't I say that I needed space? Didn't?"

"Then why did you kiss me that night? And what is this I hear about you dating someone you work with? Isn't that prohibited? And if you need so much space, why are you dating him and not me?"

Was he or was he not the most arrogant man? Why was I dating someone else besides him? I refused to answer him. I decided to pretend he wasn't there. I pulled out a mangled dollar bill and tried to insert it into the candy machine. At first it spit my dollar right back out. I let out a little curse. I tried smoothing the bill out then inserted it again and then another bill. This time it took it.

"I thought you said you weren't hungry?" I heard him pout behind me.

He was still there. I thought he'd get my message when I turned my back on him.

I just let out a sigh and pressed one of the buttons for a Butterfinger. "That's awful for you. You know?"

"And so is beer and greasy pizza," I said looking over my shoulder. I slipped ten quarters into the next machine and bought a cold Root Beer.

"All of them are bad." I walked to one of the tiny round tables and took a seat. He sat down right smack in front of me and smiled with a little-wicked grin. "If you think you are going to get rid of me by ignoring me, you're wrong. So, you may as well answer my question."

I peeled open the candy bar and took a bite. As I chewed, I asked, "Which of the many questions would you like me to answer?" I asked rhetorically. Yes, I was cranky and feeling mean. "Let's see if I remember them all? Why did I kiss you? I think I told you the answer already. You smelled good. I have a thing with odor. I always did. I was also a little more than tipsy. I am a light weight. I don't drink much." I took a very noisy obnoxious gulp of the root beer. Because I took a huge gulp, I let out a huge burp. I wanted to get rid of Jacob. I figured burping would do the trick.

Jacob just rolled his eyes, made a face of disgust and shook his head. "That's not going to get rid of me either."

Damn. "Okay, what was your other question? Oh, I remember, something about me dating someone from work and if it was prohibited. Who I decide to date is none of your business, and it is none of your concern whether it is forbidden or not. Now, why do I hate you so much?" I asked him.

He crossed his arms and leaned back into his chair. He blinked his eyes. They were the most beautiful eyes I had ever seen with long thick eyelashes. I could stare into them for hours. He had two eyebrows. Jerry had one eyebrow that extended from one end of his hardheaded forehead to the other. What did I ever see in Jerry? I couldn't remember.

Jacob's pupils dilated. For a brief moment, I felt like he was putting some spell on me. I felt slightly dazed.

He leaned forward and put his elbows on the table. He said in almost a whisper. "You are looking at me the same way you did just before you kissed me."

I blinked and leaned back in my chair to avoid any possible contact with him.

"Look Jacob. I'm not going to lie to you. You are the most attractive man I have seen in a long time. Lord knows my hormones rage when I just look at you. But you stand for everything that I am against."

His eyes darkened and narrowed into angry eyes as he looked at me. He asked in a low disappointed tone, "How could you say that? You don't even know me."

"So far what I know, I don't like. You think you can impress me with a fancy job title like Pediatrician. A job like yours apparently means you love kids. Automatically the maternal longing inside of me is supposed to kick in and make me like you. But it isn't working," I lied and continued, "Then you think you can hypnotize women with a dazzling smile, looking unbelievably handsome and smart and strong? as if a woman could just collapse into your arms and forever feel safe." I wanted to keep my guard up. I took a deep breath and continued, "You think you can control any woman. Basically, to cut it short, you're arrogant." I took an enormous bite of the candy bar and immediately took another sip of soda. Blah, I should have accepted his invitation to lunch. I already felt bloated from the soda. I needed to eat healthier. Blah? I wasn't going to tell Jacob he was right, though.

He leaped out of his seat. "Sandra Ray, you won't have to worry about me anymore. Derrick and Gina were very wrong about you. They don't know you at all. I am going to make a tiny suggestion to you. Take a good look at yourself in the mirror. I think you'd find someone who is truly arrogant staring back at you." He turned to leave but then turned back around, narrowed his eyes at me and with a smirk on his face. He shook his head as he thought of something and smiled. After a moment he said, "Your sister said you write very well. It tugged a little at my heart because I always had a particular respect for writers. I bet when you do write, you write in the first person. I also bet that when you finally do write a book, it will be about yourself." He smiled as if he just said something so profound and mind boggling. He was calm when he said, "If you'll excuse me my lunch break is over. I have to go to work on a job I worked my butt off to get."

I let my eyes follow him as he walked out of the cafeteria. I finished my candy bar. So? wait? Was he calling me arrogant? No? no... No? I don't think so. I don't go around controlling people and thinking I'm God's gift to mankind. He's such a jerk! I'll have to tell Kevin about this. Hopefully, Jacob will keep his promise and leave me alone. Write a book? Psttt. First person? Psttt... Whatever.

CHAPTER SIX: "Pass the turkey, please."

Thanksgiving came and passed. Work became a pain in the butt. Every other day we had some special sale. My department finally became busy. Women in all shapes and sizes were trying on black velvet dresses for Christmas parties or upcoming New Year's parties. I didn't mind the business because it made my workday go faster. It was the customer complaints that I couldn't take.

I had to work Christmas Eve. I didn't mind too much because I was paid time and a half for it. The store also closed at five o'clock instead of eight or nine. Just before closing time Kevin came over to me. He was wearing his usual blue denim jeans, a white t-shirt, and a Santa Claus hat. A candy cane was stuck in his mouth.

"Aren't you supposed to be locking up downstairs?" I asked him as I was placing a customer's dress in a garment bag. The customer seemed annoyed that my attention wasn't concentrated on her. I didn't care.

"Yes," He made obnoxious sucking sound from the candy cane. "But I wanted to?" He took a bite of the candy and made crunching noises, "talk to you first." His lips were glossy from candy.

I smiled a naughty smile and said, "Oooo."

The customer's face was turning red. I handed the woman the bag and said, "Happy Holidays." She didn't even bother to return the greeting. It gets to me how customers forget that salesclerks were human too. It seemed that customers thought we woke up and went to sleep solely for Robertson's Department Store, but then again, management thought the same thing. I hated retail. I really did.

"Actually, I didn't want to talk?" Kevin took the spot the customer formerly had. He glossed his lips with the aid of the candy cane and leaned over the desk, closed his eyes and puckered his lips.

I laughed. "I don't see any mistletoe anywhere."

He opened an eye then slowly opened the other one. "Okay, no pressure from me." I saw Laura from the corner of my eye. She was rushing around with a bunch of dresses in her hand. She was trying to clean up. I began to count the cash register.

"Well, I just wanted to give you something for Kissmas."

I stopped counting and looked at him. "I didn't? I? We? I didn't get…"

"I? I? I?" He mimicked. "It's okay. I just saw it on my break and had to get it for you." He pulled a long-stemmed rose from behind his back. It wasn't real. The bud was made of milk chocolate.

I blushed. "Thank you."

He had a lot of warmth in his eyes. "You're welcome. You are always welcome Sandy."

I wondered what he meant by that. We had gone out about five times since that first night in the parking lot. It was all out of fun and friendship. Twice we just went out to eat and talked. Once we went to the movies. Another time we just walked around the empty mall and window shopped after everything was close. The last time was special. I had forced him to go with me to the astronomy dome at school. Professor Rogers happened to be there that night. We looked through the large telescope and saw the Orion Nebula. Kevin and Dr. Rogers ended up having a lengthy discussion on the possibilities of aliens. They talked about how life on other planets could be insects or plants or something completely unimaginable. Dr. Rogers had ended the conversation by stating, "If Earth is the only planet with life on it, I have to say then it's a mighty lonely universe." For someone who hadn't wanted to take an astronomy class Kevin certainly enjoyed himself. I enjoyed myself just listening to the conversation. I smiled thinking about that night.

Laura interrupted my thoughts by saying, Sandy, do you mind if I leave right now? I have company at home, and I'm anxious?"

"Go ahead, Laura. It's okay."

"Thanks."

"I'll see you downstairs," Kevin said to me as he walked away with Laura. I watched them walk toward the escalator. Kevin had said something that made Laura laugh. I felt a sudden weight on my chest. The two of them would make a good couple. Laura was about six inches shorter than he was. Their hair sort of matched each other. They were beautiful. I watched them as if I would a movie. Just as they were getting on the escalator to go down, I saw something that reaffirmed that they belonged together. Kevin had very lightly placed his hand on Laura's lower back. It only remained there for a brief second but for me it seemed in slow motion.

It's a mighty big universe; I thought, why am I in it?

I finally made it downstairs. I opened my purse and of course Kevin looked inside. He glanced up at me and said, "Have a very Merry Christmas, Sandy."

"Thanks, you too," I said. I probably should have said more but didn't.

"What was that all about?" I heard someone ask when I was outside. I looked over my shoulder to find Regina right behind me.

"What do you mean?"

"Is something going on between the two of you?"

I looked through my purse. I could hear the keys jingling. "What? No, Regina. We're just friends."

"Uh, huh." She pointed a black chain at her car and pressed the button. I heard a beeping noise come from her car. "Are you sure? Does he know you two are friends? only friends?"

"What are you talking about?" I finally found my keys. They were underneath my check book.

"He wished you and only you a very Merry Christmas. And, girl, there's been some talk about the two of you? staying late after work? hanging out in the parking lot?" She opened the door to her black Mercedes. "I hope it's only a friendship."

She didn't wait for me to say anything to defend myself or at least respond to her. She climbed into her car and drove off twenty seconds later. Why was a single woman who worked in the men's department driving a Mercedes, anyway?

On my way home I thought of Kevin. But out of nowhere Jacob managed to squeeze himself into my brain. It frustrated me. I hadn't seen him since that day at the hospital. He kept his promise and never bothered me? So why was I thinking of him now?

I had imagined him sitting right next to me, and he asked me, "What do you see in Kevin that you don't see in me?"

"A lot."

"Be specific. I need to know."

"Okay, here it goes? He just doesn't talk about himself. He listens to me, and he's interested in what I have to say. He laughs."

"I laughed. I listened to you. You just never talk to me. You never gave me a chance."

"He isn't pressuring me into a relationship."

"Neither was I?"

"Yes, you were. Okay, maybe you weren't but Gina and Derrick were. They expected us to hit it off great. I'm tired of doing what is expected of me. I want to do something that is for me and not anyone else. I did everything for Jerry. I cooked for him. I cleaned for him. I gave him my heart. I woke up in the morning and rushed through the afternoon just so that I could be with Jerry right when he got home from work. I lived for him. If he wanted me to mow his front lawn in the nude, I would have done it. I had lived for him and with him for almost two years. Can't anyone understand what I feel? What I lost?"

The Jacob I had imagined looked down at me and shook his head. He remained silent sitting next to me. I parked my car in its designated spot on the street in front of my sister's home. Jacob disappeared into a tiny crack in my brain.

On Christmas Day Derrick, Gina and I went to an early Mass. At my suggestion, Derrick called the church to verify the time. The priest was young. He must have only been two or three years older than me. We were sitting in the fifth pew from the front. I couldn't actually pay attention to what he was saying because there was a baby crying in the seat behind me. The mass eventually ended, and I didn't feel any holier than when I had come in. I felt fonky? exactly the way I felt the last time? like I didn't fit in or belong there. I felt like God was shaking his head at me disapprovingly. I felt like I haven't done anything with the life He gave me yet, and I still didn't know what I was supposed to do. I felt sad and empty inside. I wished I had my journal with me. I would have tried to write down my thoughts.

After mass, the three of us drove to Los Angeles to visit Derrick's family. While we were sitting in traffic Gina announced loudly out of the blue from the front passenger seat, "I'm going on a sex diet!"

I was sitting in the back seat. Previously, my mind was blank from watching the trees pass by as Derrick slowly crept through the traffic. I was listening to the jazz music playing over the stereo and feeling my eyes fight the urge to roll to the back of my head and fall asleep. I tended to have my best sleep in the car while Derrick was driving. But I have to say, Gina's unexpected out of the blue announcement woke me up and unwillingly brought me to full attention. There were just some things I preferred not to know. Derrick seemed to have been brought out of his driving trance and said, "What?" He knew the announcement would affect him in some way. I could sense him debating whether or not he should get cranky.

"I'm going on a sex diet," Gina said again. She was looking at Derrick when she said it. She said it as a challenge.

He groaned then took a deep breath and clenched his jaw. "What exactly does that mean?"

Gina smiled then explained, "I read in a magazine that a woman lost a lot of weight from having a lot of sex. She ate whatever she wanted but had sex more than three times a day. I want to try it."

Didn't we just leave church? Wasn't that supposed to be a private conversation between the husband and wife? Why did she have to make her announcement with me in the car? I slapped my forehead with my right hand. I wished I could be at work instead of in the car with a horny sister. I could see Derrick grinning from ear to ear even though all I could see from where I was sitting was the back of his head.

"Okay," he nodded and said in a low whisper that I still managed to hear, "We can start your diet in my mom's bathroom." I wanted to hurl because I knew he was serious.

When we arrived at his parents' house, Derrick and Gina left me for a few minutes sitting on the couch. I made idle conversation with Derrick's grandmother and his cousin. "What do you plan on doing when you graduate sugar?" Derrick's grandmother asked me.

My stomach started to hurt. It was the usual feeling that I endured whenever I was asked the question. "I'm still not sure," I answered honestly.

She stared at me for a while with an unreadable expression then said, "Derrick says you work in retail. You don't see yourself doing anything more than that? You're beautiful and obviously a smart woman. Start seeing yourself doing something you love for a living. It isn't about how much money you make or how much stuff you own. It's what's in here." She pointed to her own heart. "Do what you love for a living. Be your own boss." My eyes misted a little. What do I love to do? I asked myself.

Gina and Derrick returned holding hands and smiling. Gina's hair was down. When we first arrived, she had her braids twisted in a bun on her head. I shook my head. No, they didn't do what they said they'd do. I held my stomach and tried not to hurl.

Derrick's mother cooked a file' gumbo. It was good, but it wasn't anything close to my mom's. Later in the evening presents were shoved at everyone. Christmas was finally done and over with when we were on the freeway heading home. At least I thought it was over until Gina opened her mouth and started singing. "Frosty the Snowman" off key and in her high pitched squeaky voice. But fortunately, Derrick interrupted her by singing "Silent Night". Both Gina and I were quiet to listen to him. I had to admit, brother-in-law could sing! I felt goose bumps all over. For the first time that day, I smiled.

I wouldn't have to go to school for an entire month so that meant I could put in a lot of hours at work. The week following Christmas went by without Kevin. I avoided him successfully. He didn't exactly try to contact me either.

On New Years' Eve, Adrian threw a party. I was to go straight to her house after work. Juan had planned the whole thing the night Adrian told him her parents would be out of town. He had asked one of his friends to be the DJ. He had also produced a stack of flyers and was passing them out to anyone who would take one. Adrian stopped by Robertson's earlier and gave me some flyers to pass around.

I gave one to Laura, Regina, a cute guy in the shoe department and a few other people.

Kevin was sitting in his chair with his arms crossed when it was time for me to leave. He didn't say hello to me or anything. He didn't even bother to look in my purse when I showed it to him. He just stared at me. He didn't blink his eyes once. "Aren't you going to check my purse?"

He didn't answer. He just sat there. I suddenly realized that maybe he knew that I was avoiding him. He probably also heard about the party. I didn't want him to go. I knew that if he went, he would hang around me the entire time and then people would think that we were going out. Then Gina would say something racist, and I didn't want to deal with anything like that tonight. It was about to be a new year; I wanted to start it off right.

My hand, without knowing it, reached into my purse and pulled out a flyer and gave it to him. He narrowed his eyes a little bit and then took it without saying anything. "See you there," I said and walked out. That was the first time that Kevin hadn't checked my purse. I somehow felt insulted. I knew that was how he wanted me to feel.

"Did you pass out all the flyers?" Adrian asked me.

"Yes." We were in her kitchen. I was smoothing out the tight curls in the back of her head with a straightening iron. She wanted to wear her weave up tonight.

"Sandy, this is going to be so much fun. Did you see the equipment Juan's friend brought with him?"

"He was fine, wasn't he?"

"Ooooo? Sandy. I was talking about the D.J."

"So was I." I smiled.

"Ooooo?"

"I'm almost done," I said. "Do you think this is okay to wear tonight?" I was still in the clothes that I wore to work.

"No way. Uh uh. You are not wearing that to this party. You look like an old maid in that."

I looked at one of the kitchen windows to see my reflection. Adrian was right; I looked like an old maid. I had a black polyester skirt that went a couple of inches below the knee and a big bulky sweater that covered my butt and no hint of a female figure. I did a double take at my image. "Yuck," I said out loud. I put down the straightening iron and took a closer look at myself in the window. I didn't have any makeup on. My hair was just there? there wasn't any style to it at all. Was that how I had been looking for the past couple of months? Uh uh. Not anymore. "Look at me Adrian. Your hair is nothing compared to mine. I mean really? Look at me. Let me borrow some of your clothes."

"I was waiting for you to snap out of it!" Adrian grinned.

She rushed to her mother's closet and pulled out a form fitting black dress. It barely fit me, but Adrian said, "It really fits you? yes. That's it. That's the one!"

She forced me to keep my black pumps on. Then she stuck me in the seat she had been sitting in earlier. She used a tiny curling iron and made a bunch of spiraling curls in my hair. Then she attacked my face with makeup. A few people had already shown up when she was finally done with me. Juan's friend started playing his music. It was booming. I hadn't heard music like that in a long time. It was so loud that I couldn't help but move to the beat. Some of the windows in the house were shaking. By ten thirty the house was packed. I danced with a few guys. One of the guys was a little too freaky for me. I had to leave him on the dance floor, which was Adrian's parent's living room. By eleven thirty I noticed a few people from work had showed up.

I was surprised that Gina hadn't told Jacob about the party and asked him to crash it. Gina and Derrick refused to come to the party themselves because they thought they wouldn't want me to throw the same kind of party if they were away on vacation. Kevin hadn't shown up yet. I wondered if he would ever come. I knew that I would be disappointed if he didn't. It was a minute to midnight and the DJ stopped the music to announce the New Year. I scanned the crowd to see if I could find Kevin. He wasn't anywhere. I found Laura, though. She was standing on top of the couch with a glass of champagne in her hand. I pushed and shoved my way to her. "Sandy, great party?"

"Yeah. Do you know if Kevin came or not?"

Just then the D.J. blew a whistle into a microphone, and everyone shouted, "Happy New Year!" Someone had tossed confetti. Laura screamed and then drank down her champagne in one quick gulp. I never knew she was like that. I hadn't had a drink all night. I was dancing the entire time? and looking for Kevin. Who from the looks of it never showed up.

Laura was out of it. She didn't even know her own name. I looked around. Everyone seemed to be out of it. Adrian and Juan were in the corner sucking each other's face. Why was I here? I had to leave. I had to leave now! I managed to make my way to Adrian's room. My purse and clothes were still on her bed. I quickly got out of Adrian's mother's dress and changed back into my own clothes. I grabbed my purse and snuck out of the house.

Outside, a cold breeze brushed up against my face. Goosebumps rose all over my body. I couldn't wait to get into my car. I had parked it in Adrian's driveway. Oh, no? I couldn't believe it! Someone had parked their car right behind mine. Damn, now how in the world was I going to get home?

I glanced at my watch. It was twelve thirty already. Hmm? I tapped my foot with my arms crossed. I was debating going back inside to track down whoever blocked me in or walk home. Tap, tap, tap of my foot. Think, think, think? Okay, it would be faster to walk home. I decided to walk. I only lived a couple of blocks away. It shouldn't take me too long? I was wrong? so very wrong? I couldn't handle walking to the corner. I was freezing.

A car drove past me from the other direction. A few minutes later a car just like it passed me from the other direction. It stopped then did a U-turn. I stopped walking. I wondered if maybe I should run back to Adrian's house. I could always just lock myself in her room until the party was over. The car pulled up right beside me. The windows were foggy, and I couldn't see inside the car. The door to the passenger side suddenly opened. I ran as fast as I could toward Adrian's house. I heard the driver call my name. I slowed down to a jog and turned my head. The driver got out of the car. "Sandy! Wait! It's me!"

Just as I recognized him, I felt my left knee ram into something very hard and frigid. The next thing I knew my entire body had done a complete flip in the air before it landed on a soft patch of grass. I felt great pain in my lungs. They were fighting to get back the air that had been knocked out of them. I imagined my soul popping right out of me and trying to force its way back in.

Once my breathing returned to normal, I felt pain, nothing but the pain from my left knee to the same ankle. I sat up and tried to stand. "Don't move, Sandy." Kevin was quickly by my side. "I'm sorry I scared you. I thought you recognized my car. I was trying to find the party. This is all my fault. Let me look at it."

I lifted my skirt a little bit. We couldn't see much. The only light came from the street lamp that wasn't bright. "Maybe I should call an ambulance."

"No, it's not that serious," I grumbled. "I'll be okay. I just need an ice pack or rather two ice packs."

"Are you sure you don't need a doctor?" I heard the genuine concern in his voice.

"Yes, I'm sure." I was more interested in what had caused me to fall in the first place. Five feet away from me was a fire hydrant. So that was what it felt like to run into a fire hydrant.

Suddenly Kevin burst out laughing.

I scowled and asked, "What?"

"I can't wait to tell people at work."

I smiled despite myself and started to laugh too. "Don't you dare!"

We laughed a little while longer. "Help me get up?"

"Sure."

He grabbed my left arm and pulled me gently to my feet. At first it hurt but after a while I couldn't feel anything. I just knew I would have a swollen knee and ankle for a while. "Where were you going?"

"I? I? was um?" I couldn't remember. Kevin made me forget.

"How come you weren't at the party?" Kevin asked.

"I didn't want to stay. I just wasn't in the mood, I guess?"

"Well, do you need a ride home?" I looked at him for the first time tonight. He was in black dress slacks, a long white sleeve dress shirt. He was also wearing suspenders. His hair was neatly pulled back into a ponytail. I knew that if I got into the car with him, I wouldn't be going home. The way he looked tonight and the way I felt tonight was too dangerous.

"No, I'll be fine."

His feelings were hurt. He swallowed. "Sandy?"

I started walking. "Hmmm?"

"What's going on?"

That was the second time someone asked me that. "I don't know Kevin."

"Sandy?"

I turned around. He was only inches from me. I felt something in my abdomen stir. My breathing became unsteady. "Kevin? I?" Kevin's lips were on mine before I could move away from him. I resisted him at first, but soon my mouth opened and welcomed him. My arms found their way around his neck. His hands were moving up and down my back. It felt wonderful. It felt right.

When it was over, Kevin looked at me. "Sandy," he said softly, "Do you want me to take you home?"

"I want you to take me. I just don't want to go home." Did I say that? I meant it, but it was a little on the cheesy side. I blushed. The decision was made. It was bound to happen, and we both knew it. I was ready to take our relationship to the next level. I was prepared to move on from Jerry.

Kevin looked intently into my eyes. "Are you sure?"

"Yes," I said without hesitation.

Kevin led me upstairs to his second-floor apartment in Northridge. On the drive there we hadn't spoken a word to each other. There hadn't been any reason to say anything. Now he was nervously fidgeting with his keys. He couldn't find the right one to open the door. "Are you sure you live here?"

He let out a light nervous laugh then said, "Of course." Just then the door unlocked. "You are just making me a little jumpy Sandy." He had a simple apartment with a family room, a kitchen, and a master bedroom. It resembled a hotel room. I could see his entire apartment with one sweep of the eye. His place was immaculate. I finally took a step into his apartment. The carpet was gray. He had a rose colored futon in his living room with an oak coffee table. I noticed the comforter on his bed was rose colored too.

"Would you like anything to drink?"

I looked at him. He looked back at me. "Nuh uh."

He gestured his hand toward the couch. He closed the door behind me then joined me on the sofa. "So?"

"So? He responded.

"Your place is nice."

"Thanks."

"You're welcome." My stomach was doing flip flops. I was getting hot. Not the good hot, but the bad hot. I was also getting nervous. Not the good nervous...but the bad nervous. It was a sign. I shouldn't be here. I had better leave now before I did something stupid.

"How was the party?"

"Do you have protection??"

"Yes. It's in my room?" He stood up and stretched out his hand. I took his hand and followed him into his bedroom. We made it to his queen sized bed. He pulled back the covers with one hand while he was still holding my right hand. It wasn't me in the room. It couldn't be. When I was a little girl, my mom told me that there would only be one man that I would have sex with. That man would be my husband. Yet, here I was.

We were standing by the edge of the bed still fully clothed. He gently touched the back of my neck. It was a gesture that caressed my soul. In return, I unbuttoned a few buttons on his shirt. I let my fingertips reach up to touch his bare chest. He was exquisite. The tips of my fingers lightly stroked his chest. He flexed from my touch. My hand's moved upward toward his shoulders where I succeeded in getting his shirt off. Still standing, we kissed. The clothes were in our way. It was too hot to wear clothes. It was too stuffy and unnatural to wear clothes. I pressed my body to his and I could feel him rising, anxious to greet me. We descended to the bed. I felt love in my heart. Kevin had to know that this was love. He had to. I shouldn't have to say it. It was something he had to know already.

CHAPTER SEVEN: "He's allergic to Oreo cookies."

I woke up to tiny kisses on my neck. Kevin wrapped his arms around me with my back facing him. He cradled my breasts in each of his hands, granted they were the size of ping-pong balls, but he cradled them, nonetheless. He wrapped a leg over mine. We were bare on top of the bed. It felt so right.

"Sandy," he said in a husky voice.

My eyes were still closed. "Yeah?"

"Are you here?"

"Yes."

"Good."

I love you too, I thought.

"Why?

I smiled and opened my eyes as I turned my head to face him. Did he just read my thoughts? "You shouldn't have asked that."

"You aren't going to start acting weird at work now, are you?"

I closed my eyes again. "What do you mean?"

"This past week you completely avoided me and then you didn't invite me to the party until I gave you a guilt trip. What was that all about anyway?"

I wiggled myself free from his grasp and sat up. "I didn't want this to happen. But I'm glad it did."

I bent down to pick up my sweater and pulled it over my head. "Hey," he tugged on the sweater. "Are you going to act funny around me at work now?" He asked again and sat up. I turned to look at him. His hair was out of the ponytail.

"Probably."

He shrugged. "At least you're honest," he smiled. "Hey, do you want to take a shower together?"

What was it with men and showers? Jerry always said the same thing in the morning. Jerry. I couldn't believe that I thought of Jerry. But now that he was in my mind, I might as well make a comparison. Was that a wrong thing to do? Well, I didn't think so. Kevin was great! He was attentive to all my needs. He didn't just use me to get his enjoyment. He waited until I was satisfied. Jerry just spread my legs apart, plunged in, rolled over and fell asleep. Stupid me, I thought that was the way it was supposed to be. Jerry never held me the way Kevin did in the morning. Jerry never asked me what I'd like him to do to me.

"Sandy? where were you just now?"

I blinked. "Oh, nowhere." I blushed. I had a feeling he read my thoughts. "I don't need to take a shower."

He sniffed my arm. "Yes, you do."

"No, I don't. I just took one last month?"

"You're so crazy." He laughed again. "So, we can have sex together, but we can't take a shower together? Teresa was the same way."

"What! I know you didn't just compare me to some other girl you slept with? Teresa?" My eyes popped open when I realized whom he was referring to. "Teresa! That girl from the jewelry department? You slept with her?!" He compared me to a loose floozy in the jewelry department. The girl would do it to a door knob if she couldn't find a man. Did he think of me as some cheap tramp? I stood up and slipped on my underwear and skirt. I shoved my bra into my purse. My eyebrows were meeting one another.

"Sandy, what's wrong?" He stood up and slipped on his underwear and a pair of jeans from his closet. "I know you were comparing me to Jerry."

I turned to face him. My mouth opened wide. I was trying very hard to deny it. I picked up one of his pillows and beat him with it. He raised his arms each time to block the blows. "Don't?" hit, "you ever" hit "compare" hit "me" hit "to that" hit, hit "Ho!" hit, hit, hit.

He grabbed his other pillow, and I tried to make a run for it. "Don't you ever," I felt a blow against my butt, "compare" another blow hit me across the head, "me to that asshole!"

We were both beating each other with the pillows. It ended when the pillow I was holding flew out of my hands. I grabbed the pillow Kevin was using before he could strike me again. We were both holding the pillow and laughing. "Truce?" I asked hopefully.

"Truce."

We gave each other a smooch on the lips. "Yuck, " I wiped my mouth, "boy, you need to put some mouthwash in that mouth of yours."

"I will if you take a shower with me."

"Okay."

He was shocked. We both stripped off our clothes again and took a long, long shower together. While we were eating toast and drinking orange juice, a sudden thought occurred to me. Gina, Derrick, Adrian and maybe even Juan were going to kick my butt. I hadn't called them or anything. They had no idea where I was. It was already eleven forty something in the morning. "Kevin, I have to get going. I didn't call my sister or my best friend. No one knows where I am." I had accidentally left my cell phone at Adrian's house last night.

He was disappointed but seemed to understand. A half an hour later he drove me back to Adrian's house.

Derrick and Gina were standing outside of Adrian's house when Kevin and I pulled up. Apparently, they had just arrived because Gina had her finger on the doorbell. Derrick turned away from the two-story home at the sound of Kevin's car pulling up next to the curb. He had a look of fright and worry on his face but when he noticed Kevin, it changed to a face of pure outrage. Derrick grabbed Gina's arm. She turned to the direction Derrick was pointing. He was looking at Kevin's car. Gina's jaws clenched tightly together.

"Uh, Kevin," I said before taking a deep breath and swallowed a ton of saliva. "I think it would be safer for you to stay in the car," I warned him as I unbuckled the safety belt then unlocked the door. I was about to climb out of Kevin's Mustang.

"Don't be silly, Sandy."

"Look Kevin." I pointed to Derrick; Kevin peered through my side of the window. "You see that guy heading our way?"

"Yeah, so?"

"He's my brother-in-law. He thinks of me as his little sister. Trust me. Stay in the car."

He swallowed. "He's your brother-in-law? Is she your sister?" I turned my head away from Derrick to look at Kevin. He looked surprised.

"Yes."

He looked different. He was still looking at Derrick and Gina. "Kevin?" He looked at me. His face had blushed. "What's wrong? Other than my brother-in-law about to kick both of our butts, what's going on?"

"Nothing," he obviously lied and turned away from me to stare out the front window. His hands gripped the steering wheel.

"Stay here. I'll be right back, okay?"

He didn't say anything. He just kept staring out the front windshield. Derrick was waiting for me. As soon as I got out of the car Derrick asked, "Where were you? Why didn't you call? Why didn't you let Adrian know you left the party? What's wrong with you?!" He was less than two inches away from me. I was afraid.

Gina slowly approached me. She stood behind Derrick. "Derrick," Gina tapped him on the shoulder, "let me talk to her, okay?"

"Who's that guy in the car? Is that Kevin?" He shouted in his deep testosterone voice.

"Babe, go inside. She's my sister. I'll handle this." Gina said confidently and coolly.

"I'll kick his ass if he took advantage of you, Sandy!" His fists were balled up. Gina pushed him toward Adrian's house. I was standing on the sidewalk trying to think of what I was going to say. How was I going to justify my actions? I was standing between Kevin's car and my sister.

My eyes followed Derrick as he huffed and puffed his way to Adrian's front door. Adrian and Juan were standing on the front porch watching everything. When Derrick, Adrian, and Juan finally went into the house, Gina looked at me with disgust. "Girl, couldn't you at least pick up the phone and tell us where you were? Couldn't you?"

"I'm sorry, Gina."

She rolled her eyes and bit her lower lip. "Who is he?"

I was now getting pissed off. Sure, they had a right to be angry that I didn't call last night but the way she said, "Who is he?" She made it sound as if I were a tramp. "Oh, just some guy I picked up last night. We had a wonderful time in the sack. He said he was going to give my number to all of his friends. Isn't that great! I'll be able to make a lot of money that way. I could quit Robertson's and school."

She pointed one of her long acrylic nailed index finger at me and threatened, "Don't even start pushing my buttons, Sandra Ray! You know I can still hurt you, little thing!" She shook her head and took a deep breath before saying, "I told Mama and Daddy that I would watch you and take care of you. Now tell me what you did last night." I was scared. I admitted it. I was really and truly afraid. Especially by the way she was wearing the black denim jacket and navy blue sweats. She was dressed and ready to hurt someone, namely, me.

I couldn't think of a word to say. To my surprise, Kevin stepped out of the car. He slowly approached my side. He wrapped an arm around my shoulder and extended his right hand out to Gina. "Hi, I'm Kevin."

Gina just looked at his hand, rolled her eyes and folded her arms. "What did you do to my sister?"

"Gina, I?" I still couldn't come up with anything to say. "She stayed with me last night."

"Mmmmm? hmm."

"Gina, I told you all about Kevin."

"No, you said you were just friends." She looked back at Kevin. "Are you planning to marry my sister? Now that you have slept with her?"

"Gina!" I couldn't believe her!

"I?"

"I didn't think so. My husband is pretty upset. Right now, I don't blame him. I suggest you get in your car and go home."

"No, Gina." I stood up straight. "That is something for me or him to decide." I swallowed then said. "No, we aren't just friends anymore. Not after last night. But you can't make him go away just because you can't handle it." I pointed a finger at myself. "This is my life. As messed up, as it may seem to you, it's my life. If you think this is a mistake, then it's a mistake I am choosing to make, not you."

She unfolded her arms. She had a look of astonishment on her face. I thought for sure that the next thing she was going to say was something like, 'move out of my house' or something. But instead, she looked down at her feet and was quiet. She lifted her head, narrowed her eyes as if she had a hard time seeing but looked at me anyway. "You're right. I'll let it go. Just call us next time, alright?"

I was blinking my eyes constantly. "Alright." I looked at her suspiciously. That was too easy. Somehow, she was probably using reverse psychology on me or something. That was just too easy.

Gina stood right smack in front of Kevin. They were the same height. "I'm telling you now. I don't like you. You disrespected my sister. She may not see it right now, but I do." She looked him in the eyes for ten long seconds then turned toward Adrian's house. I heard her mumbling, "Two months? less than two months and she goes to bed with him? damn? white? damn? two months? no five or six weeks? Weddin', damn it!" She slammed Adrian's front door behind her.

Kevin and I were standing on the sidewalk. He let go of me. We were facing each other. "I'm sorry," I said.

He ran a hand through his hair to keep it from falling in his face. He looked very nervous. What was he thinking about?" Um? Sandy?"

"What's wrong?" I felt my heart beating faster at every passing second. This was the same feeling that I had when Jerry was about to tell me why the "For Sale" sign was jabbed into his front lawn.

"Maybe your sister was right."

I could feel the pressure building in my throat. I could feel the unshed water beginning to sting my eyes. "What do you mean?" I crossed my arms and hugged the sweater I was wearing.

"I mean? I don't want to hurt you. I don't. But maybe we did move a little too fast."

"So now you want to dump me three times as fast? How could you?"

"I'm not saying I don't ever want to see you. I just think we should slow down?"

"How slow?"

He backed away from me a little. He rubbed his face with both of his hands. They were the exact same hands that had touched me in the most intimate way last night. "I don't know."

"Is it my sister that's scaring you or my brother-in-law?"

I had to know what I did wrong. Everything was so perfect this morning and last night. What happened since then to make him change his mind about me? If he had cared about me, neither my sister nor Derrick would scare him away.

"It's just that we barely know each other, Sandy. I didn't realize?" He let his realization trail off deliberately. He wanted me to figure it out so that he would not have to say it and seem like the jerk he was.

It took me a moment, but I suddenly figured it out. When I finally figured it out, my pupils became very tiny. "You didn't realize that I am Black, did you? That's what this is all about isn't it?" My back became straighter, and my heart turned hard.

"You have to understand?"

I moved closer to him. Each step I took toward him, he took a tiny step back toward his car. "No, I don't. I'm the same person that you made love to last night, early this morning and in the shower?"

"You just don't look or act?"

"What the exactly do I have to do, Kevin?" My eyes burned into him, his soul was ugly. I asked a little louder and angrier, "What the fuck do I have to do?" I stood grounded on the grass that was between the sidewalk and curb. "I thought you already knew my race and I thought you didn't care! So now what? Just because my skin is really supposed to be dark, but it's light you're going to throw everything away?"

He frowned. He looked down at his white Nike's that were covered with dirt. That would be the way I would remember Kevin from that day on, his white muddied Nike's. "I'm sorry. Just give me some time."

I uncrossed my arms. "You shouldn't need time, Kevin." It hurt. It hurt too much. I couldn't look at him anymore. I turned around and went into Adrian's house. I knew that inside the house were four people who truly knew who I was and loved me no matter what. Just as I reached the door, I heard Kevin's car drive off. As soon as I was inside, I closed the door, leaned against it and cried.

"Oh, Sandy," Adrian rushed over to me and put her arms around me. "What happened? Are you okay?"

"Where does he live? I'll take care of him," Juan said.

"No, you won't have to. I will," Derrick said.

They both looked like they were ready to go hunt him down and kill him. Gina was quickly by my other side. "Why don't the two of you play a video game or something? Can't you see she is upset?"

"I'm not letting him get away with using her like that!" Derrick said angrily.

Liquid was coming out of my eyes and nose. Finally, one of them realized that I was in desperate need of some Kleenex and brought me a box. Gina and Adrian led me to the dining room table. I blew my nose. I'd never blow my nose like this for a man ever again. I refused to. This would be the last time that I would lose control over my emotions and hormones.

I could hear Juan and Derrick talking in the living room. "I could get some of my friends and we could pound him. Man. We could take care of him."

Suddenly the Derrick I was accustomed to returned. "No, beating him up won't solve anything. It would make me feel better, but it wouldn't solve anything."

"That's right Derrick," Gina said. Both Gina and Adrian were rubbing my back. It felt good.

"So, what happened? When I left, I thought the two of you were going to elope or something?"

"No, the opposite," I said as my tears finally stopped, and I blew my nose one last time. I balled up the tissue paper and set it on top of the black lacquer table. "He broke up with me. I was too ethnic for him."

"See?" Gina began, but Adrian shushed her.

"Go ahead?" Adrian encouraged.

"That's it. He broke up with me because I'm black. He didn't know."

"See?" Again, Adrian shooed my sister with her hand.

"Jacob would have never?" Gina couldn't wait to start her speech.

"Jacob would have never had the chance that Kevin did," Adrian said for me "Why don't y'all let up on Jacob? She doesn't like the guy. And she just had her heart broken for the second time by a man. Running to another one isn't going to help."

Just then there was a knock on Adrian's door. A second later, the doorbell rang. "Uh oh." I heard my sister say. I looked up to see a guilty expression on her face.

"What Gina?" Adrian asked at the same time I asked, "What'd you do?"

Juan answered the door. Jacob stood on the other side. I swallowed a wad of snot and frowned. "I can't believe you, Gina!"

I just thought he'd be able to help. We didn't know where you were, so I called him this morning. He'd want to know if you were missing. He cares about you, Sandy."

"You're going to have to deal with him on your own! I'm going home."

"Now don't be rude," Gina said with her hands on her hips. Juan and Derrick were at the door greeting Jacob as he walked in.

Adrian, Gina and I stood up at the same time. "Damn," Adrian whispered, "he's fine!"

"And smart," Gina said smiling.

"Girlfriend, what's wrong with you? That's a beautifully chiseled fresh piece of meat sitting on your plate. You should put some A-1 on that baby and eat up. Damn." She was whispering low enough so that only Gina and I could hear her. Gina's eyes were wide and glazed over with a stupid smile on her face.

"See?" Gina said almost drooling.

"Yeah, I, see?" Adrian said. She looked away from Juan for a moment then back at Jacob. I could tell she was making a comparison. Everyone could tell she was making a comparison.

I had to get away from the two horny toads. "Nice to see you, Jacob. Sorry, I can't stay."

Derrick just finished shaking Jacob's hand and introduced him to Juan. As soon as Jacob saw me, his attention was focused on me. "Nice to see you too, Sandra Ray."

"Sandy," I corrected. I picked up my purse and headed for the door.

"Sandy?"

"Sandy!"

"Sandy, Sandy?"

"Sandra Ray!"

All four of them were calling me. The latter one was my sister.

She sounded more and more like my mother. I turned around and walked out of the door. Jacob was inside now. He was so comfortable there. He was making himself at home with the people I was supposed to be with. He just walked right in. I hated the fact that he appeared as if he belonged at a spot where I belonged. Kevin was supposed to be there and before him, Jerry. But neither of them was here, just Jacob.

I turned my back to them. I heard one of them call my name, but Jacob said, "It's alright. Let her go."

Yes, let me go.

I unlocked my car and drove off. I wasn't sure where exactly I was going. I just knew that I was going. I had to keep moving. My gas tank was full of gas. I had a map in my car. It was only two o'clock. Hmmm. I could be in Fresno by six or seven depending on traffic. Or I could be in Vegas by seven or eight. Hmmm. My mom or my dad?

My mom would tell me to give Jacob a try and just to forget about Jerry and Kevin. My dad would just hand me a bucket of nickels and send me to the slots.

I knew that I had to stop looking for other people to solve my problems for me. I had to start addressing them on my own. I was on the 118 freeway heading east and I had to make up my mind where I was going. I had my credit card. That was good. I had paid it off.

"Sandra Ray, you just got your heart broken for the second time, what are you going to do?" I asked myself out loud.

The answer that came to me was church. I got off at the next exit and got back on the freeway going the opposite direction.

I parked my car in the vacant lot of the church. I just stared at the building for a while. I hoped that it was unlocked. I just wanted to sit there for a while. I didn't care that I was still wearing the clothes that I had gone to work in yesterday. The same clothes that I had gone to Kevin's apartment. I got out of the car and slowly walked to the church entrance.

Inside, it was empty. Flowers were still on the altar from Christmas. The stained glass windows sent a reflection onto the front pews. I walked to the second pew. I knelt down, made the sign of the cross and prayed the Lord's Prayer silently. When I finished, I made the sign of the cross and sat back in the pew. I stared at the statue of Jesus on the cross, which was centered in the back of the altar. I was hoping to find answers to the questions that were stumbling through my mind. Was the heartache a result of going to bed with two men that I wasn't married to? Would any man ever have me after sleeping with two men? Why couldn't Kevin just love me the way I loved him? Why did God make races? No? I stopped my question. I liked the fact that there were different colors. I liked that there were differences in the world. It made the world more interesting. The best question to ask was why did God make racists?

I heard one of the doors to the church open then shut. I turned my head to find Father. I stood up and nervously headed for the door. "Hello," I said, as I was about to pass him, but he stopped me.

"Hello, how are you?"

"I'm fine," I just lied to a priest.

"I'm Father John," he stuck out his hand. I shook it.

"I'm Sandy."

"Nice to meet you. Is there something I can help you with?"

I was blushing now, "No, not really."

He searched my face but said, "Well, alright then. I'll see you on Sunday." He started to walk toward the altar.

Was that it? I'll see you on Sunday? I didn't know exactly what I had expected. I guessed? I just? I didn't know. "Father?" I heard myself call out to him. It came out loud. In fact, it echoed.

"Yes?" He turned to face me.

I just noticed that he was wearing a blue pullover sweater and had stubbles on his face. I always thought priests wore the black uniform with that white collar thing around their neck all the time. "I just wondered if you could hear my confession."

He smiled. He probably knew it was going to be a good juicy one.

He gestured his hand to follow him to the confessionals. He opened a door, and I was about to follow him inside, he laughed. "No, no, that one." He pointed to a door that was next to the one he had opened. I hadn't been to confession in a long time. I thought that since I was the only one in the church, he could just hear my confession in one of the pews, but I guessed not.

I forgot how tiny the confessionals were. They had a space big enough to kneel, and that was it. I had the option of speaking to Father face to face or sliding this shielding thing to hide. When I first entered the shielding thing was up, and I was facing him. There wasn't any way I was going to say what I was going to say face to face, forget it. "Do you mind if I pull this down?"

His eyes seemed to sparkle from my question. Oh, he just couldn't wait to hear all the garbage contained inside of me, could he? When I thought about it, it was ridiculous. He knew my first name. He knew my face. So, from now on he'd know everything about me. Did I have to do this? I mean didn't God already know that I felt awful for all what I had done?

"Sandy?"

Now, why did he have to say my name?

"Are you ready?"

"Y… yes." I made the sign of the cross. "Forgive me Father for I have sinned. It's been… um… It's been… Wait…" I used my fingers to count how many years." It's been about six years since my last confession?"

I paused to see if I could hear any reaction from Father John: a sigh, a gasp, anything. But he remained silent. "Continue, please." I knew he was on the edge of his seat just waiting to hear it.

"Okay," I took a deep breath then said, "I kind of lost my faith. I guess it's because of the relationship I was in for two years. My parents divorced without any warning after my sister moved out. I ended up moving in with my sister and met Jerry." My voice cracked a little when I said Jerry's name. "I thought I was going to marry Jerry. I slept with him believing we loved each other, but things didn't work out. But I lived with him… then I… he… he turned out to be married… then…"

I paused again. I waited to hear him breathe or something. Tears were building up in my eyes. They were waiting for me to blink so they could spill over onto my cheek.

"Continue."

I sniffed. "Okay," I cleared my throat. "I… I thought I loved him at the time. Later, I realized that I didn't love him. Even after I found out he was married, I slept with him a couple of times. I just felt bad. I knew I'd never see him again and wanted to have a good bye I'd remember. But I feel so ashamed. I feel… I don't know." I sounded awful. Was I that bad?

Father shifted in his seat. "I see. Continue."

"And last night, I went to a party and afterward a friend of mine took me home with him. I loved him? I thought I did, Father. I knew I loved him. I slept with him last night and this morning. Then he just broke up with me just a little while ago. I…"

"You're doing fine. Please continue."

"Well, that's the main thing I wanted to confess. But I also use too much profanity. I talk back to my sister when all she wants to do is help me. I exaggerate. Okay, I sometimes lie but not all the time. I just tell little lies. Let's see? I want to knock my brother-in-law out for always bossing me around… and… let me see… what else? Um…" I was trying to think of anything else bad I had done within the past six years. Then remembered one other thing and said, "I accidentally stole McDonalds about four years ago. See, I went thru the drive thru. The person at the intercom told me to pay at the second window. So, I skipped the first window and went to the second window. I was ready to pay, but they ended up just handing me the bag of food and a large Coke. I pressed my foot on the gas and took off before they realized what they did. I felt like I won the lottery or something. You know? It was free, and I was hungry. I feel bad now though and yet I kind of don't. That's bad. It wasn't my fault though." I thought I heard a giggle. Was he laughing at me? I tried to think of anything else. "Um... that's it, father."

Father let out a huge sigh. It was a little too huge for me. Finally, he said, "You had great courage to come here today." I did? Really? "You gave a magnificent confession." I did? He suggested that I come to a weekly meeting for singles to regain faith. I'd think about it. He provided a couple of other suggestions then he asked, "What have you learned from these two relationships?"

I learned that it hurts to be rejected. It hurt to be tossed aside. It hurt to be rejected because of the color of my skin. It hurts to be used for one night's pleasure. It also hurt to be repeatedly used, to be lied to by someone that I thought I loved and thought loved me. Instead of saying all of the thoughts that were roaming in my head I said, "I..."

"Try not to get so lost in the physical world. Try to find your way back to God and seek pleasure in the spiritual world instead."

I swallowed. It was a hard thing to swallow when the physical world could feel soooo good. "Thank you, Father." I stood up and left. When I was in the car, I realized I was supposed to say a prayer or something with the priest. He was also supposed to tell me to say Hail Mary's and Glory Be's, but I felt too awkward to go back and ask him for my penance.

I felt lighter already and a whole lot better. I wasn't ready to face Gina, Adrian, Juan or Derrick, though. I drove around aimlessly and listened to music for about thirty minutes. I ended up at the beach. It was cold and foggy. I sat on the sand and stared out at the ocean feeling at peace while listening and watching the wave's crash against the sand. Seagulls flew in circles above me but once they realized I had no food they left me alone. It was funny that even though I was alone it was one of the first times I didn't feel lonely. I don't know how long I was on the beach but finally, that evening I decided to treat myself to dinner and a movie. I had a date with myself. It was nice.

When I finally got home Gina and Derrick were gone. I checked the answering machine in the kitchen. There were three messages. The first one was some guy selling the local newspaper. The second one was Adrian telling me to please call her as soon as I got home because she had something crucial to tell me. I'd call her tomorrow. The last message made my day. It was also symbolic that at the same time the message began to play; I farted. "Somebody's lucky I live way out here in Atlanta because I would kick her fat black ass. You must have thought it was so funny to send me soap? What were you tryin' to say, huh? I know it was you, Gina!" Jerry went on to shout explicit words for the answering machine.

CHAPTER EIGHT: "Mind if I stay home? forever?"

I had a couple of days off from work, which I was thankful for. The problem was that on the day that I was supposed to go back, my car broke down. I couldn't call in sick either because I had used up all of my sick days. The good thing was that it was a weekend, so Gina was able to drop me off, and I could just get Regina or Laura to take me home.

"You should just get a new car," Gina said while we were on the freeway.

"Just? I love the way you say just. Maybe you and Derrick could just buy a new car, but I can't afford it."

"Oh, right," Gina said apologetically, "Sorry."

That was all we said to each other on the way to Robertson's. "Do you want me to pick you up?"

"No, Regina or Laura should be able to drop me off. Thanks."

I was nervous the entire time I was working. I knew that Kevin was working today, and I knew that he was probably looking at me with the aid of security cameras. It wasn't fair that he could spy on me when I couldn't spy on him.

I had a visitor when it was close to my lunchtime. I was taking dresses out of boxes and plastic bags when she came. She scared the crap out of me, too. She snuck behind me very quietly and said loudly, "Why didn't you call me!"

I trembled, dropped the hanger and dress I was holding. I almost had a bowel movement right there on the sales floor. I turned around to find Adrian laughing. My heartbeat finally calmed down. I cursed a few words then asked with my hand over my heart, "What are you doing here?"

"I'm here to take you to lunch."

That was the first time she ever came to visit me. Furthermore, Adrian never took me to lunch. Juan was probably out of town or something. "Me? Are you sure?"

"Sandy, I'm your best friend. I just wanted to be here for you. Besides, you have to help me pick out a wedding dress."

What? Did she just say wedding dress? It finally registered. "No? tell me you aren't marrying that fool! Are you?" I asked.

Her lips spread into a huge smile. "Yep."

"No?" I shook my head, "Don't do it? please? Don't?"

"I'm going to do it. You can't stop me."

I crinkled my nose. She was going to marry Juan. Wow.

"When is your lunch break?"

I glanced at my watch. "Forty minutes."

"Okay, then you can show me some dresses. Not too fancy cause it's not going to be a big wedding. We're going to Vegas."

"Eeeschheaseeessd," my face twisted. "Nuh uh! No, you aren't!"

"Yes, we are. We want to be married before the baby comes."

My eyebrows raised up high. She was just throwing all kinds of new news at me. She was throwing it at me with absolutely no mercy at all.

"Yep, you're going to be a maid of honor and a godmother all in the same year." She was so happy. She was full of smiles.

"How do your parents feel?"

She frowned. "They're upset, of course. They refuse to pay for any part of the wedding and told me that I shouldn't expect to live with them once I'm married."

"So, I guess they don't know the pregnant part?"

"Of course not!" We were standing near a rolling rack and three boxes that held a bunch of dresses that I was

102

supposed to have on hangers by the time my shift was over. I would work on that later. I showed Adrian a few dresses. She turned her nose up to all of them. "Maybe a classy pants outfit?"

"You are worse than my real customers."

She tried on more outfits. She didn't like any of the things she tried on. Finally, it was time for lunch. She walked with me to the third floor where I clocked out. "So where are you taking me?" I asked as we walked out of Robertson's and into the mall. I took off my nametag.

Of course, she took me to a hamburger stand. We were talking about a bunch of stuff then suddenly a thought occurred to me. "We could stay at my dad's place."

"No, you can stay at your dad's place. Juan and I will be staying at the new hotel."

I understood. It wasn't just their wedding, but it was also their honeymoon. What a cliché! Vegas? "Well, when is it going to happen?"

"In two weeks? before I start showing."

It was strange sitting here next to a woman who I knew since the third grade. Here she was pregnant, and about to get married. It might have been shocking at first but was good news. She loved Juan. Juan loved her. Oh, brother. It was too mushy and lovey-dovey cozy for me. I suddenly felt like I was suffocating. I felt sorry for Adrian. Here she was pregnant and about to get married. I got the hee-bee gee-bee's just thinking about it. Yuck, and she was marrying Juan, also known as bubble-butt, hairy-butt, stinking smelly butthead. Oh no!! I just realized something too!! Oh!! I was mad now!! Why was it okay for her to marry someone outside of our race?? He was Mexican. Why was it okay for her to marry him when it was bad for me just to date Kevin? I put my hamburger down and guessed I did more than put it down. I slammed it down.

"What's wrong, Sandy?"

103

"Nothing, I just lost my appetite." Adrian then kept on jibber-jabbering. She talked about the apartment that she and Juan were going to move into. She talked about how she would graduate a few months before the baby was due. She was one semester ahead of me. My temples were starting to hurt. Baby, husband apartment and degree? She was about to have it all. She wasn't even working. She was getting a job as a receptionist at her father's job. That was all she needed. She just needed her foot in the door, and she'd make it to the top. She would have a business degree in May with honors. I was feeling sick.

I did a quick review of my life. Twenty-three. Single. Light skinned Black, female, salesclerk, satisfactory college student? I still had no idea what I was going to do with a degree in English. I now had less than twelve months to figure it out. I couldn't see myself ever getting married. I mean, sometimes I could. There was a part of me that saw me as an eighty-year-old woman sitting on the front porch. As an older woman, I would watch my great-grandchildren, grandchildren and children in my huge front yard at a family reunion. The reality part of having great-grandchildren was that I would have actually to give birth to my children first. I was a wimp when it came to paper cuts. I couldn't imagine myself giving birth to a baby. The other half of me saw myself as a single woman who died at a young age. That was a pathetic thought, I knew.

When I thought about it, though, how could two people stay together for twenty or thirty years until death did them part? It was a prison, wasn't it? I mean seeing the same person every morning and every night? But then again, I saw my sister's face every day but that was different. Well, maybe not. I just knew that I would never depend on a man for anything. I would always depend on me. Considering I had no idea what I was doing with my life, it wasn't much to count on.

Finally, lunch was over. We walked back to Robertson's. Adrian said goodbye to me in front of the cosmetics department. She also heard about my car and asked if I needed a ride. I told her no. My car was another thing that I had to worry about.

Later that evening I was straightening up the floor, eagerly waiting for the announcement to be made over the intercom that our store would be closing soon. I was bending down to pick up a hanger when I had another visitor. This time the visitor had a deep radio voice. This time the voice didn't scare the crap out of me. This time the voice made something soothing stir inside of me. "Hello, Sandra."

"Hi Jacob," I said as I stood up. I turned around to face him.

I had a feeling that he would show up today. I knew the way Gina's mind worked. "I was told you needed a ride home." His hazel eyes gleamed. His short brown hair nicely combed back. He was dressed in tan slacks, a white dress shirt, and a brown trench coat. I couldn't place the cologne he was wearing, but he wore it the right way. He didn't drown himself in it. Instead, he put just enough on so that a woman could sense a subtle amount. So that she would want to move in closer to get a better scent of him, just like I wanted to do now.

I cleared my throat trying to get my thoughts back on track. I hadn't yet asked anyone for a ride, which was stupid on my part, considering the store closed in less than five minutes. Perhaps deep inside I was hoping he would show up. "Yes," I admitted, "I do."

He blinked continuously for a few seconds. He put his hand over his heart. "What? No argument? You mean I didn't drive all the way over here for nothing?"

I fidgeted with the hanger I was holding. "Yes, you came here for nothing. I mean, I need a ride home, but that's it. Don't expect anything from me."

He stuck his hands into the pockets of his trench coat. He nodded with a little smile on his face. "Sounds fair to me. Are you ready to go?"

"I have to close the register. I'll meet you downstairs by the men's department. That's the employee entrance and exit," I explained.

"Okay," he was about to turn around but added with a smile, "Sandra."

I was used to him calling me that. I gave him a smirk and went to the register. I watched him as he walked toward the escalator. He wasn't too bad. He knew I was watching him. He looked over his shoulder and smiled his smile again. I smiled back at him for the first time.

When I finally made it downstairs, my stomach started to hurt. I knew I would see Kevin. As predicted, there he was, sitting in his chair. He said goodbye to everyone, checked all of the women's purses. I noticed Jacob was standing outside with his hands in his pockets. I made sure that my posture was straight as I approached Kevin. I opened my purse without saying anything. His jaw was clenched. He avoided eye contact with me but peered inside my purse. I wasn't going to say anything at all but ended up surprising myself by casually saying, "Good night, Kevin."

He finally looked at me in surprise. "Good night, Sandy."

I opened the door and was outside next to Jacob. "Is that Kevin?" Jacob pointed. I turned to see if he was pointing at him.

"Yes, but not the Kevin I thought he was."

"I'll be right back." I grabbed his arm to stop him from going into the store. Kevin looked at the two of us from the inside. He swallowed, frowned then turned his head.

"No. I can deal with this on my own. Besides you aren't my boyfriend or anything."

Jacob stood still for a while with his jaw clenched. "Okay, let's go." He managed to get hold of my left hand. I tried to pry his hand out of mine, but he had a good grasp. He led me to a truck. Truck? I had imagined him driving a sports car or a luxury vehicle. He pressed a button on a black key chain that resembled Regina's. His truck chirped. He unlocked the passenger side first and finally let go of my hand.

"So do you know what's wrong with your car?" he asked as he backed out of the parking space.

"The starter, probably. At least that's what Derrick thought."

"Hopefully you won't need a new one?"

"Tell me about it." I leaned against the door.

We were quiet until we were on the freeway. "So, where would you like to go for dinner?"

"Excuse me? I? I don't think I heard you correctly," I said. I was tired and hungry, but I didn't feel like talking. I didn't feel like feeling anymore awkward than I already felt being with Jacob, the handsome and successful Pediatrician.

He laughed. "I know you're probably hungry."

"Yes, I am," I admitted. "I have some leftover fried chicken in the refrigerator."

"I was thinking more of Chinese, myself."

"Chinese won't fill me up the way fried chicken would but… okay," I gave up. I was fooling myself if I thought I could be in control of my life. This morning was a great example; my car just wouldn't start. No control. Then look at me now. I was with Jacob of all the people in my world. I closed my eyes and leaned back. I was tired.

Fifteen minutes later Jacob pulled up in front of a new Chinese restaurant. I must have dozed off for a minute because I couldn't remember exiting the freeway. He held my hand as we walked from our parking spot to the restaurant. It only took a couple of minutes for us to be seated. The lighting was dim, and it was relatively quiet with soft murmurs of conversations surrounding our table.

Since I felt I had no control, I let Jacob order the food. While we waited, Jacob tried to make conversation, but I wouldn't budge. I just nodded or shook my head at whatever question he asked me. Occasionally, I would take a sip of water.

He let out a deep, frustrated sigh. He stared at me for a while. What did he see? I wondered. Why was he here with me? Or rather, why was I here with him? "I'll take you home after this," he said in a resigned tone.

"Thanks."

Finally, we were back in the truck heading for Gina and Derrick's house. Jacob turned his radio on? loud. He had it on a slow station. Oleta Adams was singing, "Get Here". I didn't know how or why but a tear rolled down my cheek. Not a big rush of tears, no sound from my throat but a single tear. I wiped it away before Jacob would notice.

He stopped his car behind my dead car. "Thank you," I said as I grabbed my purse with one hand and the door handle with the other.

"Do you need someone to talk to?"

"No, I just need some sleep."

"I'm worried about you."

"Don't be."

"Look, all I was ever interested in was friendship. I never wanted anything from you, Sandra. I know Jerry and Kevin probably told you the same thing but not every guy you meet wants to have sex with you."

He threw me off guard. How did we get on this subject? All I said was, 'thank you.' He was supposed to say, 'you're welcome' and then I was supposed to leave. "I'm not a little girl Jacob. Don't you think that I already know that not all men look to me for a good time in the sack?"

"No, I don't. You're how old? Twenty? Twenty-one?"

He was trying to start an argument. I grabbed the handle to the door and pulled on it. "I'm twenty-three. I'll be twenty-four in April. What does my age have to do with anything thing? Numbers have nothing to do with how mature someone is."

"Why do you want everyone to call you Sandy instead of Sandra?"

What kind of question was that? I was too damn tired to listen to his stupid questions. "What does my name have to do with anything?" Why was I still sitting here and not in the house?

"A lot, Sandy is a name for a little girl. Sandra is the name for someone who's mature."

What the flying frickin-frack was he talking about? "I've been called Sandy since I was a little kid?"

He looked at me as if I just proved his very important point. "Exactly."

"Get a girlfriend, so you can leave me alone. Please." I finally got out of his truck and made my way to the front door.

Jacob rolled down his window and said, "Derrick and Gina invited me over for a barbecue next weekend. I'll see you then."

"Oh, goody," I mumbled as I unlocked the front door.

CHAPTER NINE: "I'll have mine well done?"

On Tuesday, I got my car back from the mechanics. I charged it on my if-my-car-breaks-down credit card. Wednesday through Friday I went to work. Kevin and I pretended as if nothing ever happened between us. We never went out all of those many times. We never talked during all of those long hours. We never had meaningful conversations. We didn't make love on New Year's. It never happened. It hurt me every time he checked my purse and never said a word to me. He never apologized. He never said he was wrong, never said he loved me. He never asked me to give him another chance. I tried to think of a time when Jerry may have said he loved me. He said it every time we had sex but was it real? I doubted it.

Saturday morning, I went shopping with Adrian. She was still searching for her wedding outfit. She finally decided on a white business suit. I thought she would have chosen something more romantic, but she was happy with the stuffy and boring look. It took me by surprise considering Adrian had always dreamt of a lavish dress with a long, long train.

We were about to order food at a hot dog stand when Adrian glanced at her watch. "Oh, girl, we forgot about your sister's barbeque."

"I didn't."

She shoved my shoulder then forced me away from the stand before I could place my order.

As soon as we entered my sister's house, the smell of meat on a barbeque grill entered our nostrils. I licked my lips. My stomach growled from the smell. My taste buds could taste the ribs that Derrick had just covered with sauce. "That smells so good," Adrian said smacking her lips.

Juan was stretched out on a lounge chair in the backyard. He had a beer in his hand. "Hola, mi esposa." Adrian was surprised to see him. She rushed outside and gave him a kiss. I saw Jacob sitting at the round patio table. He had some dominoes in his hands. I guessed he was playing with Derrick. Gina was in the kitchen making potato salad. "Hey, girl."

I was shocked when I saw her. Gina's braids weren't there anymore. She had her hair short? natural. "I like your hair."

"Thanks, but you know me. I'll probably get the braids again next month." She was cutting up green onions. "Why don't you go outside and play dominoes."

I took her advice. "Hello," I greeted Derrick, Juan and Jacob. I sat down at the table and reached for seven dominoes. Jacob seemed surprised. I glanced at the score pad. Derrick was leading. "Do you want a beer, Sandy? They're in the cooler right there." Derrick used the tongs to point at the ice chest.

"Not right now. Maybe later."

I saw Jacob smile a little. It annoyed me. He finally put down a domino. A half hour later, Derrick won the game. He always won.

When the food was finally ready, Jacob was the first one to grab a paper plate. Selfish, self-centered, arrogant? "Here you go," he said as he passed the plate to me.

"Oh," I gave him a half smile then said, "thanks."

Juan and Gina were having an in-depth conversation about medical school. Gina had been thinking about going back to school to become a doctor. Then Jacob joined in the conversation. Soon Derrick was putting in his opinion. Quickly Adrian and I made our own conversation. We were talking about school starting in ten days.

Out of the blue Juan asked, "Jacob, would you like to come to our wedding?"

I almost choked on a rib bone. I had barbeque sauce all over my fingers and on the side of my mouth. I was completely enjoying the meal until I heard that question. Adrian was sitting next to me and asked, "Are you okay?" I nodded my head as I took a sip of root beer.

"Sounds good to me," Jacob answered with a grin.

"You can stay with us. We're staying at my dad's house. I'm sure he won't mind one extra person," Gina suggested.

"Gina, don't you think you should talk to Dad about it first?" I asked with a glare.

Jacob wiped his hands with a napkin. "Don't worry about it. I have a friend who lives in Vegas. I'll just stay with her.

Her? He has a friend who lives in Vegas. It was a she. Okay, no problem. I didn't mind. We weren't going out or anything. Psst? her? What kind of crap was that?! Gina dropped her fork and looked at me. What? What did she want from me? I ignored her and took a quick sip of my soda again. When I lowered the glass, I found Adrian staring at me too. What? What was I supposed to do? Beg him to stay at my father's house? No, I don't think so.

Derrick wrapped an arm around Gina. Juan wrapped an arm around Adrian. Jacob was sitting across from me. Were they trying to say something to me? I mean, was this a conspiracy? I was the only female who didn't have a man's arm around them. Jacob was the only male who didn't have his arm around a woman. His arms were inviting. They looked strong and protective. Yeah, but Kevin and Jerry's arms were just as strong and protective and look what happened!

"Ready for some pie?" Derrick asked.

Everyone agreed to it.

I was so full! I was sure I was going to explode. Someone else exploded before me, one of those silent but violent ones; the kind that was hazardous if you lit a match at that particular moment. No one said anything. No one waved his or her hands either. No one got up to get away from the stench. They all just sat there. Well... I wasn't going to take it! "I'm going inside. It's too cold out here."

"Yeah, me too," both Adrian and Gina said.

It had to be Juan. It had to be. Derrick would never fart like that. I was sure that if he ever did fart it would come out smelling like potpourri or something. Jacob was out of the question too. But then again, it could have easily been Gina.

The men followed us into the house. We all threw away our paper plates. We found our way into the family room. Oh, goody. We were going to have one of those conversations: one of those comfy-cozy group conversations, one of those let's gather around and talk. Gina and Adrian were sitting on the couch, and Derrick and Juan sat in front of them. Both Gina and Adrian started to massage the guy's shoulders. Both Derrick and Juan started to move their heads from side to side. They groaned some more. It was starting to get on my nerves. "If you guys don't mind, I'm going to my room."

"Yes, I think I'll go home too," Jacob said. He must have started to feel uncomfortable too.

"We were going to play a few games?" Gina said.

"You guys go ahead. I really should be going." Jacob stood up. "I'll see you guys next weekend." He waved to everyone and was out the door before anyone could stop him.

I was still sitting down. All four pairs of eyes stared at me. "What?"

They all shook their heads. "I'm going to my room now. I'll see you guys later." I hurried off to my room and closed the door. A few moments later I heard Juan and Adrian say goodbye to my sister and brother in law. Moments later I heard Gina and Derrick giggling, and their bedroom door closed. They were going to boink. I shivered.

I wondered when my sister was ever going to have a baby. I knew she wanted one. I wondered what was taking them so long to have one.

I started to think of Jacob. We would have beautiful children together. We would have three. I was sure he wanted them since he was a pediatrician. He'd be a good dad. He was so caring. Wait, what? Where did the thoughts come from? Stop it! I had to shake myself out of the thoughts. Geesh? I never wanted a man's children before? Not just one but two or more! I could visualize what they'd look like! I fanned myself and shook my body? Jacob? Yuck? Stop it.

Pretty soon my eyes rolled to the back of my head, and I was knocked out. I woke up to the sound of the doorbell. It freaked me out too. It was pitch dark, and I couldn't remember falling asleep. I couldn't remember climbing into bed. The doorbell rang again. I remembered that Derrick and Gina were in their room. They wouldn't be opening their door until tomorrow morning, and they more than likely didn't hear the doorbell. I glanced at the red glow coming from the alarm clock. It was only eight thirty. I fell asleep before ten o'clock! That was a record for me.

I slowly got out of bed and turned on my light. The doorbell rang one more time. I heard my sister's big mouth. "Sandy, could you please get the door!"

"That's what I am trying to do," I mumbled. I finally made it to the front door. I flicked on the porch light and looked through the peek hole. The person's head was big. It wasn't his head that was big but his nose. He had beady little eyes and long hair. I hated the peek hole. I could never tell who was really on the other side. The peek hole always distorted people. I gave up the guessing game. For all I knew, it could have been a guy with a machine gun. I opened the door anyway.

114

I gasped when I realized who it was. The long hair should have given him away. No one else I knew had long hair like him. "Kevin?"

He looked into my eyes then lowered his head. He raised his head again. "I want to apologize."

Finally, did he realize that he loved me? Was he asking me back? Should I take him back?

"I want you to know that in the short time we saw each other; you became one of my best friends."

My left hand was holding the door open. I nodded. His eyes looked down at the ground. "I never meant to hurt you. I was so surprised to find out that... I just want you to understand? I can't do it?"

"What? You can't do what?

"I can't go out with you."

My blood pressure rose. "Kevin, first of all, I already know that you could never go out with me. I'd never consider taking you back. Second, we already had this conversation. Why did you come over here? Did you want to break up with me and hurt me all over again? The first time wasn't good enough for you or what?"

He looked at me with sorrowful eyes. "I just wanted you to understand."

"I don't understand, Kevin. I'll never understand." What did I see in him in the first place? "Bigotry is something I will never understand."

He shoved his hands in his pockets and said, "I'm taking the morning shift. You won't see me at work anymore. I?"

I shook my head and frowned. Finally, I admitted in a low hurt voice, "I loved you, Kevin. I forgot about Jerry, and I loved you instead." I looked into his eyes intently. I wanted to see something that resembled the true caring inside of him. I wanted to see something that would reflect good, kindness and love inside his soul.

"I?"

"Goodnight." I closed the door on him before he could open his mouth one more time. I looked through the peek hole to see him wipe his eyes. Was he crying? I hoped so. He turned and walked to his car. I turned off the porch light.

The following morning the phone rang loudly next to my ear. I picked up the phone on its second ring. "Sandra Ray, please tell me why you're visiting your father but not the woman who brought you into this world?"

Of course, it was my mom. "Mom, how are you?"

"I'm fine, now answer my question."

I rubbed my eyes. I yawned a real yawn. "Adrian is getting married."

"What? Wow!" Then she at once returned to her offended tone, "Why wasn't I invited?"

"Because it's in Vegas, and I know you wouldn't want to be near Dad."

"Your father and I are still friends, Sandy. In fact, he came over during Christmas."

I was shocked to hear that one. Why wasn't I invited to spend Christmas with them? Now I was offended. "It's going to be at that new hotel at two o'clock on Saturday. You are more than welcome to come."

"Good, I'll be there. So how are you doing?"

"Not good, Mom. Someone just broke up with me again."

"Oh no. Was it that Jason or Jon guy that Gina was trying to fix you up with? He sounded like a nice guy from what she was telling me."

"No, it wasn't him. It was a guy I work with. But you'll meet Jacob at the wedding."

"Jacob, yeah? That's his name. Are you two going out?"

I shifted beneath the sheets. I was on my back now. "No. We are just friends? barely."

I heard my mother make a snort. Gina made the same kind of sound when she disapproved of something. Just then Gina burst my bedroom door open. Her hair was sticking up every which way. I hadn't seen her like that in a long time. She was wearing one of Derrick's white dress shirts with her cleavage bursting free. "Who's that? Is that Mom? I want to talk to her."

"Hold on, Mom. Gina wants to talk to you."

I handed Gina the phone. She plopped herself down on my bed. She would have sat on my left knee if I hadn't moved it out of the way quickly. "Hi, Mom!" She was quiet for a while then all of the sudden she burst out laughing. She started pounding her sock covered feet on the carpet. My bed started shaking. She laughed some more. "She should, huh?"

What was so funny? I sat up and scratched my head as usual in the morning. My lips were swollen. Gina laughed again. "Adrian said the same thing. Sandy needs to? huh?" More laughter.

I got out of bed. I couldn't sit here and listen to her laughing at something my mother said at my expense. I put on my robe and slippers then headed for the kitchen. Even in the kitchen I could hear her laughing. I made pancakes and bacon for the three of us. When Gina and Derrick finally entered the kitchen, both of them had huge smiles on their faces. There had to be a conspiracy between them. They were just way too happy.

CHAPTER TEN: "Are you really sure you want to do this?"

The drive to Vegas was a long one. I was in the same car with Derrick and Gina for five hours. The first hour they yelled at me because I had refused to ride in Jacob's truck. They made me feel guilty, but I just couldn't imagine myself being confined in the tiny space of a truck with Jacob the entire ride to Vegas. I still couldn't understand why he couldn't ride with us in Derrick's car. "Don't you get it, Sandy? He wanted to be alone with you. Well, I'm telling you one thing, you aren't riding back with us on the way home."

We had to stop every half hour because Princess Gina needed to either go to the restroom or she was hungry or thirsty. She was a pain in the butt. "I want some ding-dongs."

"You are a ding-dong," Derrick grumbled. "We should have been there by now. I bet Jacob and Juan are already there." Never the less he stopped at the next rest stop and bought the highness a package of ding-dongs.

My dad was standing outside watering his lawn. He had a beautiful house. It was one story, three bedroom house. It wasn't big, but yet it wasn't small either. He had a tiny kitchen but since my dad didn't cook much, it was okay. Everything was white: the tile on the countertops, the floor, and the walls. He told us to leave our shoes by the door. I had a good look at my dad. He had several more gray hairs, and he was thinner than the last time I saw him. At least he wasn't bony.

We stood in his white living room, on the thick white carpet. "Come on and give me a kiss, girls." Both Gina and I hugged and kissed Dad at the same time.

"Aren't you going to say hi to me?" I heard my mom's voice.

Gina and I turned around at the same time. I was surprised to see her. I thought she was going to stay at a hotel. I wondered if they were planning on getting back together. Gina rushed up to Mom and gave her a huge hug. Mom was the shortest one in the family at five feet two and a half inches tall. Dad was six two. As soon as Gina was through it was my turn. I hadn't seen either of my parents in a year and a half.

Derrick was standing by the white leather couch. Dad turned around, shook Derrick's hand and patted him on the shoulder. The two of them started talking about Gina. My mom and sister started talking about Adrian. I found my way into my dad's kitchen and poured myself a tall glass of water. When I rejoined, the group Mom asked me, "What time is the wedding?"

I could have sworn that I had told her already. "At two o'clock." We had left at eight o'clock in the morning. It was already one o'clock. We had to hurry up and change then rush to the hotel chapel. I still couldn't get over the fact that Adrian was getting married in Vegas.

"Did you bring some nickels?" Dad asked.

"No, we'll just trade when we get to one of the casinos."

My dad wrapped an arm around my mom. They looked happy together. I couldn't help but think they were going to get back together. Dad showed us to our rooms. I closed the door and changed into the jade pants suit that Adrian had selected for me. I was about to put on the matching jade high heels when I remembered Dad didn't want any shoes to be worn in the house from fear of messing up his white carpet. So, I carried them with me to the front door then slipped them on as I was walking outside. With the heels on I was almost as tall as my dad. Mom wore a pink chiffon dress. Dad wore a dark suit and tie. Derrick wore black pants with a white silk shirt. Gina wore a brown pants suit.

119

We piled into my father's Oldsmobile. I sat in the middle in the backseat in between Derrick and Gina. I felt like I was a kid again. The Golden View Hotel was shiny and gold. It was at least thirty floors high. To look at the hotel at one forty in the afternoon was blinding. I wondered how the windows were colored gold. It seemed weird.

At the chapel, we stood in line waiting for Adrian and Juan's turn. Juan was perspiring. Adrian was biting her lower lip. Adrian's mother and father appeared to be statues. I didn't think they would come. Juan's parents were beaming. They always loved Adrian and were eager to make her an official part of the family. Too bad Adrian's parents didn't feel the same about Juan. Maybe that was why Juan was sweating. Jacob had taken a seat in one of the chairs in the back of the chapel.

Finally, it was Adrian and Juan's turn. Tim James and I walked up with Adrian and Juan. Why did Juan choose Tim as his best man? He could have asked someone else besides the red headed, freckle faced jerk. Everyone else joined in the back of the chapel. During the five minute quick ceremony, I closed my eyes and tried to give Adrian a telepathic thought. "Don't do it? Don't do it? Don't do it? just because you are pregnant, it doesn't mean you have to marry him? don't do it? don't do it?"

"I do?" No!

I opened my eyes and found them kissing. Afterward, Adrian gave me a hug. "Thank you, Sandy. Thank you for being here."

"You're welcome." I can't believe you did it! I wanted to say.

We all went out to eat at the hotel's restaurant. Everyone was talking and laughing and smiling. "Sandy."

I looked up from my fruit salad. I was chewing on a huge grape "What?" I wasn't sure who called my name, so I said it to everyone at the table.

"Ready to hit the slots?" My sister asked.

"Forget the slots. I'm going to the draw poker machines," Mom said.

Juan's mother was trying to make conversation with Adrian's mom, but Adrian's mom wasn't budging. Adrian's parents needed to get an enema because they were just too uptight! So, their daughter married Juan. She could have done worse. At least she was marrying someone who loved, cherished and adored her. He was also very intelligent. Wait? Did I just defend Juan? It was time for me to get away from the table. "Yep, I'm ready to hit the slots. Let's go."

Gina and I stood up and grabbed our purses. My mother quickly followed. I wanted to change into some jeans and a T-shirt, but I knew Dad wouldn't want to drive back to his house so that I could change. Why did I dress up anyway? The ceremony was so quick it didn't matter how I was dressed.

I realized as Gina, and I walked away from the rest of the crowd that I hadn't said two words to Jacob. He didn't say anything to me either.

The very first slot machine I went to paid off with twenty-five nickels. From then on, I just fed the machine. I sipped on Pina Coladas and Mai tai's. I lost Gina and my mother after about two hours. At around eight o'clock I put my last nickel into a slot machine. I cursed when nothing came back in return. I felt a little light headed? no tipsy would be the right word. I walked around the blinking lights and golden carpeted hotel-casino. I could hear the sound of change hitting the metal tins of the slot machine. I loved that sound.

I saw an older woman hogging three slot machines at the same time. I saw a girl who must have only been sixteen getting carded. People were dressed so differently here. Some were dressed in evening wear. There were a couple of guys in tuxedos. Other people were wearing ripped up jeans and tank tops. I wandered around and tried to find at least one person that I was related to. Where was Gina? Where was my mom? Gees? I was getting hungry too.

I ran into Mom at one of the draw poker machines. "Are you ready to go?" I asked, a little doubtfully.

"Yes," Mom said, as she deposited her last quarter. My family did not know how to gamble. We never knew when we were supposed to stop. I always came to Vegas with the attitude that I knew that I was going to lose. I knew I was going to lose big. That was the main reason I stuck to the nickel machines. Imagine what I'd lose if I went to the dollar machine? no thanks!!!

My mom got off of the stool and grabbed my hand. It felt warm. "So, tell me how you've been. And don't say okay."

We strolled through the casino searching for Gina. "I don't know, Mom. I see Gina and Derrick and now Juan and Adrian? Then I look at you and Dad. I can't see myself marrying anyone. I know I've only been in two relationships but I?"

Mom placed her other hand over my hand, which she was already holding. "Sandy, don't compare yourself to other people, especially with your father and me. Your father and I married out of love, and we divorced out of love."

"What?" I was utterly confused. We passed the blackjack table.

"You might not understand until you have kids, and they move away?"

"I didn't move away Mom," my voice was shaky and cracking, "You two moved away from me. You didn't give me the chance to move out." I never realized I was angry. I felt abandoned. I felt as if I were dumped. Both of my parents dumped me onto my sister and sped away. I knew I was supposed to be mature about it? Maybe even appreciative that my sister took me in, but I was angry. I felt like I had no control over my life. I just kept going on from day to day? going and moving with the flow of things but not ever getting the chance or opportunity to make or create my own waves. At the same time, I felt a tremendous amount of guilt or feeling of failure because I couldn't live on my own at twenty-three years of age.

"In a couple of years you would have," my mom mumbled sadly. She didn't even look at me. We didn't look at each other really. We kept walking, and she was still holding my right hand with both of her hands. "We just wanted two different things, and we didn't wish to hold each other back. Anyway, we get along even better now than when we were married. Marriage is hard. We are both independent-minded people, and we were both tired of needing permission from someone to do what we wanted to do. Sandy, do you have any idea what it is like to have worked all your life and not be able to do whatever you want? To have to keep answering to someone else? It's hard. Call it ego, call it pride, call it selfishness? call it being fed up? I just felt like I earned the right to do what I wanted for a change. I love your father, and I always will. There has never been any question about the love we have for each other."

"You do?" I finally looked at her. Her eyes were glistening, and she looked into my eyes hoping to see understanding. She wanted me to forgive her for leaving my father. I stopped walking, and she stopped too. We were standing in front of the gift shop. "Do you think you two will ever get back together?" I asked.

"No," she said without a moment's hesitation. "We both like where we are living. We both like our arrangement."

"What kind of arrangement?" I asked, suddenly feeling a little queasy.

She smiled wickedly. She and Gina had the same smile. "He decided on January, March, July, September and November."

I shook my head and narrowed my eyes. I had no idea what she was referring to. I didn't have to say anything because she knew I didn't understand. "Those are the months that he visits me, and I visit him on the other months. We stay with each other for a few days and then go away from each other for a while. We never get lonely, and we never get bored."

So basically, they were having an affair with each other. My parents were weird. I didn't like the whole idea. I guessed my feelings were expressed on my face because my mother patted my hand and said, "All that matters, Sandy, is happiness. We are both getting older and have different things we want to do on our own without having to answer to someone else. We want to spread our wings a bit and fly. We're happy."

I shook my head. They were weird. Give me a break! Happiness. They just used each other for sex and then went on with their lives. Sex. That was all that mattered. Jerry. He left his wife in Georgia and then just used me to satisfy his sexual needs. Kevin? He was a hard one to figure out but at the end that was all it was about… sex… Wasn't it? No? no? Not with Kevin. I shook my head. If he weren't a racist, I would still be in love with him. I could almost feel his touch, his hug, his kiss… his love inside me.

I felt numb. I felt my heart beginning to break all over again. I felt this numbness all over my skin. I scratched my arm with my nails but couldn't feel the scratch. Every once in a while, I had that feeling of numbness on my skin. It seemed to happen during really high-stress sad moments in my life. I sometimes wondered if at that moment or those moments my soul had escaped my body and was trying to find someplace more comfortable and suitable to land. Like my body was this great disappointment or discomfort for my soul, so it had to leave for a little while.

My mom had her right hand on my arm. I saw that her mouth was moving, but I couldn't quite hear or understand the words that were coming out of her mouth. I hadn't felt her touch until now either.

"Sandy?" she asked with her voice full of concern.

I blinked my eyes as if awoken from a trance, "Yeah, mom? I'm sorry. I'm okay. It's just a lot to take in."

She removed her hand from my arm and her expression softened, "Okay, why don't we talk about something else?" She suggested. Immediately, she asked, "So how's school?"

"I don't know because I won't start again until next week."

"How's work?"

"Fine."

My mom sighed heavily and turned to go into the gift shop. She seemed to have given up her attempt to have a conversation with me. Instead of going inside the shop, I opted to stand around to see if I could see Gina. I finally spotted her fifteen minutes later. She was carrying a small bucket of change and wandering around. She was probably looking for us. Instead of calling out to her I just kept watching her. I wanted to see her get frustrated from trying to find us. As if she knew I was watching her she turned her head and looked at me.

"Mom's in the gift shop. Are you ready to go?"

"Yep."

"Good. My feet hurt." I was still wearing the high heels that I had worn for Adrian's ceremony.

I was in my pajamas and stretched out on my bed or rather the bed my dad let me use. I was content reading a new romance novel. After reading for an hour, I got bored and frustrated.

I was in Vegas, and I was bored! Could you believe it! I got out of bed and slowly opened the door. All of the bedroom doors were closed, and it was quiet. I quietly sauntered into the kitchen and turned on the light. The kitchen was bright. It was two o'clock in the morning.

I wondered if Adrian was awake. I decided to call her hotel room to find out. Thankfully she was the one who picked up the phone. She sounded sleepy when she answered.

"So, how's the married life?"

"Sandy?"

"Talk to me Adrian?"

"Girl, it's in the middle of night?"

"We're in Vegas. We aren't supposed to sleep." I plopped myself on top of my father's kitchen counter. I knew that if he saw me sitting on it, he'd chew me out. I heard Juan say something in the background in Spanish. He was mad at me now.

"Look I'll call you later. We're tired." Click.

How cold! How inconsiderate! I just reached out to my so called best friend and she hung up on me. She would have never done that when she was single. She was changing already.

I was still bored. If I weren't so afraid of what my father would do, I would have taken his car and driven back to the casino. But the fact was that I was still afraid of my dad? especially when it came to his possessions. The only thing that was left for me to do was to go back into my room or watch television.

I decided to go back into the room. This time I turned off the light and stared into the darkness. I wondered what I was supposed to do. What was I expected to do with the life that I was given? See? I hated it when I was bored and wide-awake because I always started thinking about stupid stuff! Like, Life. Damn. Maybe if I closed my eyes and counted backward from one hundred, I'd fall asleep. I

126

closed my eyes and started counting. When I reached forty-nine, I knew it wasn't going to work. I got back out of bed and almost tripped over my suitcase as I was searching for the light switch. My fingers felt for the tiny stump of the switch and flicked it on. I pulled off the plain pink comforter from the bed and dragged it with me to the family room. I turned on the television. I flicked through all the channels and discovered my dad had the Playboy Channel. I rolled my eyes then pretended as if I was about to throw up. I kept flicking through the channels. I finally decided on the Discovery Channel. I was hoping they would show something that would put me to sleep. I ended up watching an hour of a man explaining how he caught a big fish. I changed it again. It was going for three thirty. I switched to MTV. I knew I'd be awake; I might as well enjoy myself. I let out a frustrated yawn and lay down. I stared at the screen, and it started to get blurry.

I woke to the smell of coffee and the sound of my mother's laughter. When I opened my eyes, it was way too bright. I couldn't remember where I was for a moment. I looked up at the ceiling and saw the white walls and mirrors. Oh, yeah, I remembered. My leg was hanging off the side of the couch. I sat up. I found Mom and Dad standing in the kitchen. Dad was the first to see me. Oh, crap! Did I forget to turn the television off last night? I found that it was off. Good. Leaving the television on was one of my dad's most hated little things.

"Sandy, would you like a donut and some coffee?" My dad asked me holding a mug in his hand.

"Sure," I was still lying on the couch. Gina and Derrick strolled into the family room and then into the kitchen. They were already dressed in jeans and T-shirts. Gina had a booty bag around her waist. She was ready to go back and lose more money; I was too. I finally got up and dragged myself into the kitchen. I was the only one still in pajamas.

I grabbed a jelly donut. Instead of coffee, I had a nice cold glass of milk and sat down at the small glass table. My mom sat next to me. "So how did y'all do yesterday?" Dad asked. Even though he hadn't lived in Louisiana in decades, his southern accent would still come out every once in a while. He leaned against a cabinet and sipped some more of his coffee then took a bite of a sugar donut.

"I won one hundred twenty at blackjack," Derrick smiled.

Gina's eyes popped open. "You did?"

He nodded, still smiling.

"I lost," Mom said.

"Same here," I finally said still smacking on the donut.

There was a light tap at the door. My mom looked at my dad the way she always did whenever someone called or visited. Dad was always the one to answer the door. He sighed, placed his coffee mug on the counter and walked toward the front door. I heard the door open. "Hi, Jacob, glad you could make it."

I was contentedly munching on my jelly donut. Some of the jelly spurted out of the donut and landed on my chin as I bit into it. My mom's eyes were wide, and she shook my arm to get my attention. "Sandy," she whispered, "He's here?"

"Yeah, I know," I said, knowing what condition I was in. Jacob had already seen me in my worst, physically and emotionally. I took a sip of milk. She wanted me to somehow sneak into my room to get beautiful for Jacob.

Gina and Derrick had already stood up and were in the living room chatting with Jacob and Dad. Mom stood up to join them. I finished my donut and finally stood up too. I didn't know how my mother expected me to sneak into my room. I had to walk through the living room just to reach my room. I didn't care if Jacob saw me anyway and Jacob knew that I didn't care what he thought of me. In fact, as I passed through the living room, I let my presence known.

128

"Excuse me, Jacob. I'll be with you in a moment. I have to change. Put a hat or something on to cover up my frizzy hair." I mimicked my mother. Jacob laughed a genuine laugh. Gina rolled her eyes at me. Mom did her best to ignore me.

In the room, I rummaged through my suitcase to find something decent to wear. I settled for another pair of blue jeans and the same rose-colored shirt I had worn when I first met Jacob. I also decided to wear a pair of silver hoop earrings. I tried to comb my hair, but the comb got stuck. When I tried to yank the comb out of my hair, part of it broke off and flew across the room. I gasped as it hit the wall with a loud thwack. I fingered through my hair in hopes of finding the remains of the comb. I found it. The problem was I couldn't get it out. I opened my door a little and yelled, "Gina!"

I could hear them talking. "Gina!" There was a little bit of silence. I called for her again. Then I heard Derrick say, "I think your sister is calling you."

"What?" I heard her ask loudly.

"Come here!"

"No." I heard her continue with whatever she was talking about.

I had my limits. I wasn't going to walk out there with a piece of a comb stuck in my hair. "Please!" I shouted.

I heard my mother mumble something to Gina. Finally, Gina's feet stomped down the hall and into the room I borrowed from Dad. "What?" She pushed the door wide open and had he hands on her hips.

I raised my eyebrows and twisted my mouth to the side. "Look," I pointed to my hair; specifically, to the piece of purple comb tangled in my hair. My sister's face went from an annoyed expression to one of pure delight. She placed a hand on her stomach and laughed. "Stop it. Help me?" She was still laughing. Mom heard the laughter and walked in. She too started to laugh. I had two laughing hyenas in my room, and half of comb stuck in my hair. I tried to pry it out myself since they were busy laughing. Dad and Derrick heard laughter and walked in. Soon Jacob followed when he heard four members of my family. I was so embarrassed. "Okay, now that everyone is happy, could one of you please help me get this thing out of my hair?"

Derrick and Dad had walked out of the room. Gina followed her husband with a hand on his shoulder. I glanced at Jacob. He looked confused. He probably wanted to laugh but was holding it in. My mom shooed him away then closed the door "This is just like when you were five years old, and you tried to comb your hair." My mom wiped the water from her eyes. "Sit down." I sat down on the bed. I felt her fingers mingle through my hair. I could feel the comb slowly finding its way out. "So why won't you give Jacob a chance?"

"Because he's arrogant, and I don't like him."

She continued to finger through my hair. "He seems like a gentleman. He certainly sounds better than that security guard you were dating. He sounds better than that Jerry."

"Why do you think he's better than Kevin? You never even met him?"

She finally pulled the comb out of my hair. "Anyone who breaks up with my daughter is a jerk. On top of that he's a racist."

We were both quiet for a minute.

"Just try to be Jacob's friend. He's worth friendship, Sandy."

"I am. We are friends," I lied. Or was I? In a weird kind of way, we were friends. I just didn't think I could be friends with a guy like Jacob. He was so unbearably handsome, smart and a true gentleman. I felt like I had to have my guard up around him, especially now that Kevin squashed my heart. I thought I could trust Jerry and Kevin, how could I possibly trust a good looking, educated, successful man that could have any woman he wanted?

My mom grabbed a brush that was sticking out of my purse. "Mom? mom? what are you doing?"

She had her arm aimed at my head. "I'm going to brush my daughter's hair."

No!!! I couldn't get the word out fast enough. She began pulling and yanking my hair. The gentleness she used when getting the comb out of my hair was gone. I held my scream in as she pulled and tugged at my hair. She noticed I had a jar of hair gel in my opened suitcase. She put some gel on her palm then rubbed it into my hair. She managed to pull all of my hair into a neat and extremely tight ponytail. I was already starting to get a slight headache. I stood up. My mother bombarded me with a hug. "I love you, Sandy."

My throat strained. Those were the words I needed to hear. I wished, though, that a man would say those words to me and mean them. "I love you too, Mom." I returned her hug.

We walked into the living room together. I was expecting someone to make a joke about my hair, but no one did. Instead, they continued their conversation, something about Iowa. "Are you sure it's something you want to do?" Gina asked. Her question was directed at Jacob.

"Yes." Jacob looked somber. They all looked serious. My mom and I looked at each other. We had no idea what they were talking about.

"I'll explain everything later," Jacob said to Gina. Then he looked up at me. I was worried. I wondered if Jacob was okay. I could sense that something was very wrong. It was just something about him that told me something wasn't right. He seemed heartbroken. Our eyes locked for a few brief seconds. I tried to find the answer to his unhappiness, but his eyes refused to give me the answer I was looking for.

"Are we all ready?" Dad asked.

Every pair of eyes turned to look at me. "What?"

"Are we ready to go hit the casino?" My dad asked me specifically. Oh, I understood? They had all had been waiting just for me.

"Yes," I said with a nod. As I nodded my head, I felt the silver hoop earrings brush against my neck.

"Let's go.

Outside I surprised everyone, including myself, by climbing into Jacob's truck without an invitation.

"It's about time," Gina mumbled.

CHAPTER ELEVEN: "So maybe you're right..."

"So, how's your friend doing?" I asked Jacob, trying to
make some form of conversation.

"She's doing pretty well."

"Is she originally from Vegas or did she move here?"

"She moved here."

Okay. Now look who was the one who didn't want to
talk. Unlike him, though, I could take a hint. If someone
didn't feel like talking, I didn't attempt to make him or her
talk. The rest of the short drive to the main strip was in
silence. Jacob parked his truck next to my dad's car in the
Tropicana's parking lot. Everyone agreed to meet in the
parking lot at four o'clock for dinner. Again, Gina, my
mom and I headed in our own direction away from the
guys. We walked to a couple of small casinos and gambled
there. We were given a plain white glove at one of the
casinos. It was a glove for the right hand, the hand that
pulled the arm of the slot machines. I was on my third
Corona at one of the casinos, and I was flying. My mom
was too. I noticed that Gina hadn't drunk any alcohol. In
fact, she hadn't been drinking for the past month or so.

While I was losing more money, I kept thinking about
Jacob. What was wrong with him? Why did he seem so
sad? I had to find out. Then I ordered another Corona. I
started to think about Adrian and Juan. I wondered if they
were enjoying their honeymoon. I hoped they were.

Four o'clock finally rolled around. Gina and Mom
forced me away from a machine that I had won one
hundred and fifty nickels from. I printed out the money
receipt from the machine and walked to the cashier
window. I could use the money to buy dinner or at least
part of a dinner.

I was tired. Gina, Mom and I had been standing in the
parking lot for ten minutes waiting for the guys to show up.

Finally, when they arrived, we all argued about where we were going to eat. Ten minutes later, it was agreed we'd go to an all you can eat buffet at the Tropicana since we were right in front of it.

I was eating buffalo wings when Derrick said, "Everybody, Gina has an announcement to make."

I stopped chewing on the chicken wing. Mmmm… it tasted so good; the hot Tabasco sauce dripped from my lip. I needed a napkin to wipe the juice from my mouth. I felt a piece of the chicken in between my teeth. With my tongue, I tried to pry it out. It took a lot of muscle to get it out. I was still trying to work it out with my tongue when Gina made her announcement.

"I'm pregnant." My stomach immediately did a flip-flop and started to burn. Just the way it did, when we were little and something great, happened to Gina, and it always meant me being left out somehow. Gina was in the limelight as always: The golden child, the one who had her life together.

"Oh, my?" My mom's eyes started to water. Derrick's face beamed with fatherly pride. He even sat a little straighter. He'd make a great dad. Lord knew he fathered me enough. Dad and Jacob patted Derrick on the back and congratulated him, such a manly thing to do. I rolled my eyes. Dad took a deep breath. I finally got the piece of chicken out of my mouth and took a huge sip of Pina Colada. Jacob glanced at me. His hazel eyes were filled with wonderment. I felt butterflies in my stomach. Did I just take part in a little daydream in his mind or something? Why did he make me feel squirmy and mushy inside? With just a look, he made my body do things they weren't used to doing.

I finally forced myself to congratulate my sister and brother-in-law. Gina looked so happy. I was feeling a little sick. I thought the Pina Colada and Buffalo wings weren't mixing too well. My mom scooted her chair closer to

Gina's, and they started talking about babies. Dad began to lecture Derrick about raising children in these times. I scooped up my fork and jabbed lettuce leaves and a tomato. As I was chewing, Jacob was watching me. I glanced down at my plate and continued to eat.

"Do you mind if I take Sandy away from the table?" He asked the group. I noticed he didn't call me Sandra. I swallowed the lettuce and tomato I had been chewing on. No one bothered to answer Jacob's question. They were too busy talking about Gina and the unborn baby.

"I'm taking her to see my friend perform."

Finally, my dad answered. "Sure, go ahead, Jacob. Have a good time."

What about me? I wanted to ask. Instead, I scooted my chair back. Jacob was at my side in a flash. He must have known that I probably couldn't stand up. He helped me out of the seat and wrapped an arm around my waist as I stood up. He didn't let go of my waist either. He kept his hand there and let me lean on him. "Where are we going?"

He made a face and covered my mouth with his hand. I guessed I had alcohol on my breath. "We're walking to the Golden View Hotel." Everything was too wavy for me to walk. I was leaning on him.

"Honey, I can't walk all the way to that hotel. That's like? Like? What? Two miles away? It will take us a half an hour or more to get there."

"You need the air, and it's only a mile. You shouldn't mix your drinks, Sandy. You're going to feel sick."

"Going to," I said, I held my stomach. "I already feel sick. Oh, no…" I felt a wave of nausea come over me. I had never felt like this. My feet were thick and slippery. No, they were numb. I couldn't feel my feet… or my tongue…We made it outside just in time. I threw up on the sidewalk. I was about to stand up when another wave overtook me. I was glad I was away from the rest of my family so they couldn't witness my embarrassment to the family name. I should have known better. Beer, Mai Tai's and Pina Coladas? I think there were a couple of shots of tequila in there somewhere too. Yuck. I wouldn't be drinking for a while. One more dose of hurling spewed out of me. I felt better but still sick. People were walking past me holding their noses. Some were laughing and pointing at me; others were shaking their head in disgust, and others looked as if they felt sorry for me. I couldn't tell what Jacob's expression said because he stood behind me holding my ponytail away from my face. He handed me his handkerchief from his back pocket. Wow, I didn't think men still carried handkerchiefs in their pockets anymore. It seemed it was only something my dad did when I was little. I wondered if Dad still carried one. I'd have to ask my him later.

I groaned. "Why do you keep seeing me at my worst Jacob?"

"Hmmm? If this is your worst you must have a wonderful life," he said.

I finally stood up straight then turned to look at him. "You need some water," he said looking into my bloodshot eyes. "Then in about an hour I'll get you a coke." We walked into a little market, and he bought me a bottled water. I wanted to throw up just from looking at fluid. "Drink it," he demanded.

"I took a sip," I could feel it run down my throat and through my belly. It felt good and yet gross at the same time. I wasn't sure if it was safe to drink anything, but it turned out to be okay. I was getting feeling back in my tongue. But it felt swollen, dry and cottony. I drank more water. We began walking again to the hotel his friend was performing at. The air did feel good. Jacob was so nice. He held my hand as we walked. His other hand in the pocket of his pants. We finally made it to the hotel. As it turned out, his friend was famous. She was very famous. Jacob told me that he would introduce me to her after the show. She was so down to earth and friendly. Fortunately, Jacob had bought me breath mints and given me a handful before we were introduced. I probably still reeked of alcohol and vomit, but I was beyond caring.

We walked back to his truck after the show and Jacob drove me home. Home. It wasn't my home. It was my dad's home. Where was my home anyway? I felt the car stop. I realized Jacob had just pulled up in the driveway. Jacob climbed out of the truck then rushed over to the passenger side. He pulled open the door for me. I climbed out and wrapped my arm around his shoulders. He was a strong for a short guy. "Sandy, you're going to have to go straight to bed."

I felt like I was already sleeping.

"Do you have the keys to the house?"

I pointed to my purse. Dad had given me a spare key yesterday when I first arrived. Jacob searched through my purse and finally found the keys. He unlocked the front door. "Will you be okay?"

I blinked lazily and managed to say, "Yes."

He was about to turn around and leave me. I grabbed his arm. "Jacob, you do know I rarely drink? Right? I am having a?"

"I know?" He knew.

"Thank you."

He smiled. This time he didn't let his perfect teeth show. He smiled with his lips together. He was so handsome. Why did he have to be so handsome? And smart on top of that? Gees?

"Oh no, you're getting that look in your eyes," he said with panic in his voice.

"What look?" I asked.

"Like you are about to kiss me." He backed away from me. He was right. I wanted to kiss him, but I was starting to feel sick again. "Go to bed. I'll check on you afternoon tomorrow. Okay?"

I was going to throw up. "Okay," I said quickly and rushed inside to the house to go to the bathroom. I heard the front door close. Jacob must have closed it. I leaned over the toilet and threw up. I threw up a few more times. Finally, I felt like I had thrown up all that there was to throw up and crawled into my bedroom. I was asleep as soon as I was on the bed.

My head hurt. It was pounding. My tongue felt more swollen than it had last night, and my throat hurt, and it was dry. I felt as if my brain was dry, and it was expanding every time my heart took a painful beat. To make matters worse, my mother and father were staring down at me as soon as my eyes managed to pry their way open. My parents had a look of disapproval on their faces. Mom held a bottle of Tylenol and Dad held a Coke. My mom shook two pills out of the bottle and handed it to me. I popped the two pills in my mouth and took a swig of soda.

"I hope you feel awful," Dad said as he watched me take another sip of soda.

"So do I," Mom said as she crossed her arms.

"I do," I remembered Adrian saying the same words a few days ago.

"Good," my parents said in unison.

"We're going to a few shows with Derrick and Gina. Hopefully, you will feel better by the time we get back. We'd like to have a nice barbecue later. Juan and Adrian will be coming over."

I took another sip of soda and leaned back against the headboard. "If you still feel bad, you can stay for another day," my dad offered.

I shook my head, which was a big mistake because it made the pounding in my head worse. "I have to work tomorrow night," I explained to Dad.

They both walked towards the door. "We'll see you later," Mom said as she closed the door. They were going to hang out together. Mom and Dad looked so happy. They weren't together anymore, but they were happy. They still loved and cared about each other. Maybe they were happier. Maybe they would be okay.

I was feeling better at around three o'clock. I was stretched out on my dad's couch and sipped on some Lipton iced tea. I flipped through a copy of Jet magazine. I heard a knock on the front door. A moment later I heard it open. I hadn't realized I left it unlocked. Jacob strolled into my father's living room. "Hi."

"Hi," I couldn't believe he just casually strolled into the house as if he owned it.

"Can we talk?"

"No," I said then sipped tea.

He ignored my reply of course and said, "I'm worried about you." He strolled over to the couch I was so leisurely occupying. He made it obvious that he wanted to sit down, but I wasn't going to willingly move my legs.

"Didn't I tell you not to worry about me?" I asked. He looked down at me. He grabbed both of my ankles and lifted them up so he could sit down. He plopped my legs down on top of his lap.

"You wanted to kiss me last night."

"So."

"Why?"

"Are you going to ask me that every time I kiss or when I want to kiss you? I wasn't in the right frame of mind."

He interrupted me, "Sandra, I just want you to be careful. You don't even know me and already you've kissed me."

I blushed from embarrassment. I raised the magazine up so I wouldn't have to face him. So?"

"You've been in two too many bad relationships. Sexual that I know of. One you didn't know he was married and the other you didn't know he was a bigot." He had his hands on my shins. Even though I was wearing jeans, I felt like he was touching my bare shins. "I just think you have a habit of leaping into relationships before you get a chance to know the person for who they are. Did you ask them if they were tested for sexually transmitted diseases or anything?"

I only heard the part about Kevin and defended him. "Kevin isn't a bigot!" I yelled the lie. Why would I even want to protect Kevin? What was I doing? Why did I always fight Jacob? Then his questioning my sex education offended me. "I'm not a complete idiot Jacob. Despite what you might believe I don't just leap into bed with the first guy who appears to be interested. I have only slept with two men in my life. Jerry and Kevin. Yes, I drilled them on their sex health and yes, they put a condom on." I was so mad, but my legs were still on his lap. My argument went back to Kevin. "Kevin isn't a?"

"He is a bigot if he broke up with you because you are black," Jacob said not letting me finish my denial.

I couldn't think of a rebuttal. I knew very well Kevin was prejudice.

Jacob gave my shins a gentle squeeze. We were both silent for a while. I was trying to hold onto my anger, but it wasn't there for very long. Finally, Jacob said, "When I first came over to meet you, I wanted to meet this incredible young woman that Derrick spoke so highly of. He always bragged about you as if you were his daughter or something. He also kept begging me to meet you."

Did Derrick keep bugging Jacob to meet me? My blood pressure rose a notch. "Derrick told me he showed you my picture, and you said you wanted to meet me."

He gave me a tiny smirk and shook his head. "No, he showed me your picture then asked me to meet you."

"Oh," I sipped some more tea. That certainly changed things a bit.

"I thought I'd meet you once and one time only to get Derrick off my back."

I blinked, "Oh."

"But something told me that you needed someone. Not a boyfriend, just someone. That's all I wanted to be? someone."

"Oh." All of this was hard to take in. Jacob was telling me that he was rejecting me. I wasn't sure I could handle a third rejection, even if it were him.

"Sandra, I want you to watch yourself. Don't run to a man just because you're unhappy. Don't expect a man to rescue you. You've got to make yourself happy first. You've got to be happy with yourself and don't compare yourself with other people all the time."

What he was saying made a lot of sense. I was getting annoyed, though. "What makes you such an expert or… or… philosopher… or… um… a shrink? or whatever on my life?" I sputtered out with a small groan. I had been perfectly content sipping my tea and reading Jet before he strolled in.

"Because I've been watching you. I listened to what Derrick and Gina said. I know they want the two of us to hit it off. We both know that and honestly, a part of me was hoping we could hit it off. You are a smart, attractive and funny woman. I know you don't need a relationship right now, though. Especially not with me," he said pointing to himself.

I wasn't sure if I should be happy or not. Was he complimenting me or putting me down? I took another sip of tea and waited for him to say more.

He smiled. It wasn't a happy smile but more of a cynical smile. "Are you happy?"

What kind of question was that?

"Are you happy with school and work? Are you satisfied living with Derrick and Gina? Or is there something more that you want?"

He was making me feel depressed. I didn't know what I wanted out of life. Why was he asking me so many questions? He looked into my eyes. "Don't continue to do things that make you unhappy. If you're unhappy being a salesclerk, quit now?"

"That's easy for you to say. You have a job. Not just a job but a real career. You have a degree, and you're a doctor for crying out loud!"

"Okay, maybe that was a little too hasty. But just don't stay there any longer than you have to."

"I know that."

"Good."

We were quiet for a while. I stared at his profile. He looked as if he had more to say to me but didn't know how to say it. "What is all this about?" I finally asked.

He took a deep breath then said "Promise me that you won't rush off to the first man you meet. And don't hold back on the things that you really and truly want to do."

I finally lifted my legs off of him so that I could sit up. "You are acting as if you are saying this big profound goodbye speech." I narrowed my eyes. I was hoping I could hear what he was really trying to say.

"I decided to go to move back to Iowa."

A gasp escaped from me. So that was why he looked so sad yesterday. "Why?" I was stunned. He had just moved out to California. I placed my right hand on his back and began to rub it.

"People out here are too distant." Meaning me in particular. "People in the city don't bother to get to know their neighbors. I need people around me. I'd go crazy if I stayed here in California too much longer. I don't care how much more money I would make by staying here. Besides, I miss my mother and sisters."

I thought about Derrick and Gina's neighbor and how I never visited her after she had her baby. I was still rubbing his back. My mind was tumbling. I was trying to think of something to say. I realized though that nothing that I would say would matter. Suddenly none of my so-called problems mattered. The entire time I had thought Jacob was the arrogant one. When all along, it had been me. I was the selfish, self-centered one. Jacob was right all along. I was arrogant. I hadn't bothered to get to know any of my neighbors since I had moved into Derrick and Gina's house except for Jerry. I hadn't bothered to get to know Jacob.

We sat there for a while, holding each other. I needed to wake up and see what was here in my arms. He saw me at my worst. He always came when I needed someone, even though I wasn't the one who called him. I was obviously attracted to him, and he just said he was attracted to me.

"Don't go," I said in a panicked whisper.

He stiffened up a bit. "What? I thought you would be the first to escort me to the plane." He laughed.

"Look, I'm sorry for being such a... a?"

"Female dog? Arrogant? Mean for no real reason? Attitude all the time? Not giving me a chance at all?" He waited for me to answer but then said, "I would use the b-word, but I know you would start going off on me and right now? I like and appreciate the peaceful side of you." He smiled that smile of his.

I shook my head in denial, then smiled and admitted, "Yes, I am sorry. Did you already make plans to leave?"

"No, I had just decided this past week. I was going to tell the hospital this upcoming week."

"So, stay. Stay at least for another month or so and let's go on a few d? a? few? a few dates and get to know each other." I said it as fast as I could and then swallowed hard. My eyes were glazed from the unexpected tears that wanted to be shed. I didn't want him to go anywhere. "Okay?" I asked.

"What?" He obviously couldn't believe what he was hearing. "Where is this coming from?"

"Just want you to see how wonderful California is. Besides, my family adores you. You can't leave, or they will think it was all my fault and they'd never speak to me again."

He smiled. "I was hoping you would ask me to stay." I wasn't sure, but I thought I detected a little bit of a wicked grin. I started to wonder if I was set up. He could have easily been lying about moving. Gina? Somehow this had Gina's name written all over it.

CHAPTER TWELVE: "Mind if I ride home with you?"

It was time to leave Las Vegas and get back to reality. I gave my parents a big hug, big enough to last a couple of months for the next time that I would see them. My mom stayed behind. She said she would stay for another week. I wondered if she was euphoric with the arrangement she spoke of. I didn't want to comprehend it but the other day I could see that my parents were truly happy. They were each doing what they wanted to do, but they also spent time with each other. I thought though that at their age they would need each other more. I thought they would not want to be alone so much and so far apart. I tried not to think about it so much. I realized and accepted that my parents were only human too, and they were individuals with their needs. I couldn't control them just as they couldn't control me.

I tossed my belongings in the back of Jacob's truck. Ever since our conversation on my dad's sofa, we were pretty much inseparable. It seemed to shock everyone, especially Gina. Jacob offered me a piece of gum as I climbed into his truck. "Are you trying to tell me my breath stinks?"

"Yes, I am," he said too seriously and too quickly.

I frowned then held my hand up to my mouth and puffed out a breath. Wow! It was pretty bad. I forgot I had onions on my ham sandwich earlier. I had already packed my toothbrush and was too lazy to pull it out. I took two pieces from him.

"Are you ready to go back home?" Jacob asked. Was he losing patience with me? It sounded like it.

"Yes."

We were finally on the road. "You know Jacob. You know a lot about me, but I don't know much about you. We have about four hours to kill. Tell me about yourself."

"You know I am not used to you being nice to me," he said looking at me suspiciously.

"So, are you going to start talking or do you want to sit in silence the whole trip?" I smirked.

"Gees. What do you want to know?"

"Okay, how old are you?" I asked.

"Twenty-eight."

"Not bad," I said with a nod while trying to think of my next question. "Hmmm? what kind of women are you accustomed to dating?"

"I don't have a type. I mean I need to be at least mildly attracted to them physically, and I need to be able to connect with them on an intellectual basis."

"What about spiritual?"

He seemed shocked that I asked. He was quiet for a moment. "For dating, I don't think spirituality is a necessity but… for marriage? It would have to be a requirement."

"Why is that?" I asked.

"I want to be married in a church and it would have to be for real. I just think marriage is sacred and holy."

"Okay, if you feel that way, what are your views of premarital sex?"

He took a deep breath. "See? That is where I have a problem, and a lot of other people have a problem. Personally, I wish that I had waited until I was married before I had sex, but I didn't. At the same time, if you are going to marry someone, I think you should have sex with them a few times to be sure you are sexually compatible."

"I agree with that. I was raised to believe that I would only sleep with one man, and that would be my husband. But then here in Vegas, I found out that my parents are having an affair with one another even though they are divorced. I still can't get passed the divorce and now they are telling me they are having an affair."

"Your parents are still in love, though."

"You think so too?"

"Yes, I can see it in their eyes."

"Do you think they will get back together?" I asked a little earnestly.

"Who can tell?"

"I hope so. Anyway, let's get back to you." I crossed my feet and crossed my arms. I felt relaxed. Jacob was an easy person to talk to. "How many woman have you dated and slept with?"

"I have slept with three women."

"Three?" I asked suspiciously.

"Yes, three. The first was a high school romance. The second was a summer romance after high school, and the third was my ex-fiancé."

"Fiancé?" I asked, shocked.

"Derrick never told you?" he asked casually.

"Nope," I said, somehow my feelings were hurt.

"Yep, I was going to get married to someone I met in college. Well, she cheated on me a little more than a few times. Things didn't work out. Sometimes you have to go through a few bad relationships before the right one suddenly appears.

"Did you date a lot?" I asked.

"Yes, a lot. Have you been dating lately?"

He glanced away from the road for a moment to take a look at me. He was wearing a heather gray t-shirt and jeans. He looked so relaxed. He gave me a little smile. "I've been trying to date a beautiful young woman, but she kept blowing me off."

I gave him a half smile. "Sorry."

He reached for my hand. "It's okay."

I didn't let go of his hand. It was warm, not sweaty. A tingly sensation shot up my arm and to my chest. I took a deep breath. "So how many sisters do you have?"

"Three."

"Older or younger?"

"Older."

I pretty much drilled him all the way until we reached Gina and Derrick's house. We held hands almost the entire time. He parked the car in front of Gina's house, and we sat for a little while in his truck. Finally, he said, "Okay, Sandy? I don't want there to be any lies between us especially since we are finally developing...a... a thing."

"A thing? Is that what you call this?" He could tell I was getting a tiny bit upset.

He raised his hands up in defense. "I don't want to say relationship because I don't want to scare you away." His mouth tweaked to the other side, "I don't have to be honest if you don't want me to be," he said.

I crossed my arms and narrowed my eyes, "Yes, be honest," I said challenging him. My guard went up, and he knew it. It was a defense mechanism.

He took a deep breath. "I wasn't planning on moving. Gina talked me into telling you that, so you would give me a chance."

I just shook my head and then laughed. "I had a feeling. Just don't lie to me anymore. I can't be in a dishonest relationship."

"Okay," I knew he meant it. "You have a beautiful smile and a cool laugh."

"I do?"

"Yeah, you do." He leaned towards me. My heart raced. Jacob was only inches away from me. He closed his eyes, and his lips touched mine. My eyes finally closed, and my mouth opened to welcome him. Our arms were around each other. His kiss felt so right. He was so right. This whole entire time… He was right.

EPILOGUE- Two years later

I checked the mailbox, nothing but junk mail. I wobbled my way back inside the house. I was glad the nauseous phase was over. Even though Jacob dealt with patients on a daily basis, he couldn't handle seeing me throw up. I rubbed my belly and felt the baby give me a sharp kick. I couldn't wear my wedding band anymore because I was swollen from head to toe. No matter how big I got, Jacob continued to love me anyway.

I entered the house and passed through the living room and finally wandered into a tiny room, a room that was considered to be mine. It was my office. I sat in front of the computer. I had finally figured out what I was going to do with my degree in English. I read the words that were staring at me on the screen, "I was watering the front lawn. I was just standing there with the hose in my hand and letting the water go where ever it wanted to go?" I smiled.

If you've enjoyed reading this novel, please leave a review on Amazon and/or Goodreads!

Amazon:
Amazon.com: Sandy Times eBook : Lumas, Giselle: Kindle Store

Goodreads:
Sandy Times by Giselle Lumas | Goodreads

For more books by Giselle Lumas, here's the link to the author's page on Amazon.com:

Amazon.com: Giselle Lumas: books, biography, latest update

www.ingramcontent.com/pod-product-compliance
Lightning Source LLC
Chambersburg PA
CBHW070749120626
46557CB00002B/512